HOW IT ALL

Began

FOR THE

Baron

by

Tabetha Waite

This novella is dedicated to all the readers who asked for Cassie and Gregory's story. I hope I was able to deliver a perfectly romantic tale, as that is always my one true wish.

Chapter One

December 20, 1804
Ashcroft Hall
East Sussex, England

"Lord Gregory is coming *here* for Christmas?" Twenty-year-old Cassiopeia Brumhilda Agnes Mildred Ashcroft paced back and forth in front of her grandmother who had just informed her of the news. "Doesn't he have his own home to go to?"

Isabel Ashcroft, the Dowager Countess of Rockford, frowned at her in disapproval. "That is rather ungracious of you, Cassie." She stroked her hand down Sir Pugglesworth's back. She seldom went anywhere without her prized pug. "His parents are going to Bath this year, something to do with his father's constitution." She waved a hand. "Besides, your brother invited him here, and you know that his presence is positive for Orion. They were quite inseparable until Lord Gregory graduated from school two years ago. Since then, I've felt your brother's loss."

Cassie sighed, before slumping down on the settee; her blond curls dancing around her shoulders. "It's just that I don't get to see Rion very often." She defiantly crossed her arms over her chest.

"After this school term is over, rest assured, he will be here to bedevil you on a regular basis," Isabel pointed out.

"I wish he could have invited Roarke instead," Cassie grumbled. "At least he doesn't do his best to annoy me when he's here."

Isabel pursed her lips together. "I'm sure Lord Gregory has matured. You haven't seen the boy in three years. Don't be so quick to judge his character. Perhaps he's changed."

"I doubt it," Cassie said sourly, but seeing that another lecture might be forthcoming, she rushed to add, "but since it will make Rion happy, I will do my best to be...nice." She gritted her teeth on the word. "I just wish it seemed more like Christmas. It's entirely too mild for this time of year. At this rate, I won't even get my yearly sleigh ride!"

Isabel's lips turned up at the corners in the semblance of a smile. "It won't be all bad. Besides, you still have your art room in which to seek refuge, should the young baron-to-be's presence become too much of a struggle." She patted the pug's head. "And don't forget that I'm inviting a few of your cousins to Ashcroft Hall to help celebrate the holidays. If all goes well, you won't be alone until after Twelfth Night, after which Gregory will be preparing to leave."

Cassie stood with a sigh, but not before she bent down and gave her grandmother a light kiss on her weathered cheek. "You're lucky I love you so much, Gram, or I wouldn't be so easily manipulated."

Her grandmother's blue eyes twinkled. "Of that, my dear, I have no doubt."

***

Two days later Cassie was in the front parlor working on some embroidery when she heard the sound of an approaching carriage.

Her movements instantly paused, and she shoved the needle in the middle of the purple coneflower she'd been working on.

Rion was here! Her joy dimmed somewhat when she recalled who would be traveling home with him, but that didn't keep her from jumping to her feet and flying into the foyer.

The butler had already opened the front door, and she craned her neck trying to get a glimpse of her brother. Naturally, Rion could be a rapscallion when he chose, but they had always had a special bond. When she'd been nine, and Rion only six, their parents had died in a carriage accident. In spite of the tragedy, they realized how short life could be. However, once Rion was sent to Eton, that bond had been stretched, but she was determined not to loose it entirely.

At the first glimpse of that familiar, dark head, Cassie squealed and brushed past the butler. "Rion!" she cried.

Instantly, his seventeen-year-old head snapped up and he grinned in that wonderfully charming manner, the one that would likely stop some lucky woman's heart someday. Or break it.

"Cass!" he shouted in return as he opened his arms wide. She instantly crashed against him, feeling her eyes well with moisture.

"I've missed you dreadfully," she said with a sniffle. She pulled back and inspected him from head to toe. "I swear every time you come home you are more of a man than when you left."

He winced, although the blue eyes that mirrored her own danced with merriment. "You're not going to get all weepy on me, are you, Cass?"

"I might," she returned with a stubborn tilt of her chin.

"You haven't changed a bit, Lady Cassie." A deep voice drawled from behind them. "At least," he amended, "Your charming demeanor hasn't."

Oh, yes. *Him.* Cassie barely refrained from scoffing when she turned to face Lord Gregory Dawson, the future Baron Ambrel. But the moment her gaze lit on him, she found her jaw going slack.

Three years wasn't a particularly long time, but it had changed the boy she had known into the handsome, young man standing in front of her. While he still had the same sandy hair and green eyes that she remembered, he had gotten taller and his frame had filled out considerably. He had a day's worth of golden stubble on his strong jawline and for a moment, all she could do was stare at the changes that had been wrought.

In the temporary silence, he gave her a perusal of his own, although she knew what he would see. Her blond hair was pulled back from her face and left to hang down her back, tied with a simple blue ribbon. Her day dress was white with small blue flowers and the breasts beneath her stays were still rather disappointing, in her opinion. She suddenly wished she'd taken a bit more care with her appearance, for she felt like a child in the face of that imposing stance.

"Lord Gregory." She offered the tiniest curtsy possible, and then turned her attention back to Rion, only to find that he'd disappeared.

Cassie clenched her fists, irritated that she'd allowed herself to be so distracted by that infuriating presence. She spun on her heel and found her brother in the foyer with their grandmother. The sight of the two most special people in her world together instantly brought tears to her eyes.

Unfortunately, a rumbling voice behind her ruined the

moment. "Rather touching, isn't it?"

Cassie instantly stiffened and turned to narrow her gaze on Lord Gregory. "What are you trying to say?"

He shrugged, coming to stand beside her. "Nothing. Only that it's good for Rion to have such a steady foundation."

She tossed her head. "How would you know? You've only known Rion since he was thirteen. I've known him my entire life."

He turned his steady green gaze on her, looking infinitely wiser than she remembered. "I know more than you might think, Lady Cassie."

With that, he bowed and walked away, leaving Cassie feeling rather unsettled.

***

Since they had arrived on a relatively mild, sunny afternoon, the boys decided to go fishing on the estate pond. Cassie refused to be left behind, so she gathered her things, tied her bonnet on her head, and marched off after them. She felt as if she was an annoying sister intruding on *their* time, instead of the other way around, and it made her resent Lord Gregory's presence even more.

Gregory eyed her bamboo pole skeptically. "I never took you for a fisherwoman, Lady Cassie."

"Perhaps you don't know as much as you think you do, Lord Gregory," she returned primly.

While she had intended to put him in his place, tossing his earlier words back at him, she frowned when he threw back his head and laughed richly. She caught a glimpse of the strong column of his throat, his green eyes twinkling in amusement as she quickly looked away. "You still possess that razor sharp tongue, I see."

"You have no idea," Rion muttered. In turn, he was rewarded with a sharp glare from his sister.

They were halfway across the manicured lawns when Rion suddenly slowed to a stop. Cassie followed his gaze to the short iron fence that surrounded the family cemetery. She swallowed tightly. "Do you want to—?"

"No." Rion interrupted rather curtly. He continued toward the pond.

She felt an ache in her chest as she watched his stiff stride carry him away from the plot where their parents were buried. She couldn't remember the last time he had visited their graves or even allowed himself to grieve, if he ever truly had.

"Give him time," Gregory said quietly. "He's had a lot to deal with—"

Cassie spun on him. "You don't have to tell *me* what he's been through, Lord Gregory. I've felt their loss as well."

When she would have left him, he stopped her with a light hand on her arm. "I didn't mean any disrespect. I was only pointing out that Rion was forced to grow up earlier than the rest of us. The responsibility of his title has dragged him down for a long time."

She sighed heavily, the fight leaving her. She gave a brief nod. "I know."

He released her. "Come on. If you're lucky I'll teach you how to tie a proper lure."

Cassie felt her lips twitch in the face of that smile. "Perhaps it will be the other way around and I shall teach *you*."

***

Gregory watched the sway of Cassie's hips as she sauntered away from him. He shook his head with a snort. Rion's sister had always been a spitfire as long as he'd known her. As an only child, Gregory had always enjoyed his visits at Ashcroft Hall, because he felt as though Rion was the brother he'd never had.

Cassie, on the other hand, had *never* felt like a sister.

For years he'd been infatuated with her, and while he had never told Rion how he felt, he suspected that his young friend saw a lot more than he let on.

Unfortunately, that was what worried him. From the first moment he'd met Rion at Eton, he had been intelligent, a student with lots of potential, but as the years passed and his friend had matured, Gregory had noticed a steady decline in not only Rion's studies, but also his frame of mind. He had become more closed off and subdued, choosing to push others away rather than make new friends. Gregory had considered` confiding his concerns to the dowager during his visit, but then he didn't want to make Rion feel as though he'd betrayed his trust. Even so, when he'd received Rion's invitation to spend the holidays in Sussex, he thought this might be the chance he'd been waiting for to help Rion deal with the pain of his past.

But then, his plan would work only if he wasn't too distracted by the fair Cassie.

***

"You're cheating."

Cassie had sat with her pole in the water for over thirty minutes without a single bite, while Gregory and Rion had five fish between them.

"How do you imagine that?" Rion asked, perplexed.

"I don't know." She shrugged. "Perhaps you're using special bait to coerce them onto your hook."

Rion rolled his eyes as he took his pole and moved farther down the bank. At his departure, Cassie turned her attention on Gregory, who had taken a break from his catch to tie a new lure on his line. She had noted the pile of flies made of feathers, fur, and thread that he'd withdrawn from a small pouch he'd carried in his jacket pocket when they'd arrived. She looked at the rather pitiful worm on hers.

"Could you tie one of those on my line?"

Gregory glanced up, his surprise evident. "Sure."

She handed her pole to him and watched his steady masculine hands remove her bait and replace it with his homemade one. He was so focused on his task that she couldn't help but smile. "You're so serious," she teased.

He glanced up with a grin that caused her pulse to skip a beat. "I take fishing *very* seriously," he returned, and then he handed her pole back. "There. That should take care of your problem."

Cassie hated to admit when she had been bested, but after she threw her line in the water, from which she had a nice fat fish lying on the bank fifteen minutes later, she was forced to concede defeat. "I admit it. You're a better sportsman. At least when it comes to fishing. Now a fox hunt, on the other hand…" She let her words trail off meaningfully.

Gregory merely snorted. "We shall have to see about that someday."

"Indeed," Cassie grinned. "We shall."

***

Nearly an hour later, with a sizeable catch between them, a gust of wind blew across the bank, causing the temperature to drop several degrees. Cassie immediately shivered in her cloak. Gregory still sat beside her in companionable silence, although now his eyes lifted to the sky and the darkening clouds on the horizon.

"It looks like the December winds are preparing to blow in."

As Gregory began to gather up his supplies, Rion jogged over to them, his string and pole at his side. "A storm is brewing on the horizon. We should get back to the house."

They all took off toward the manor. Just as they went inside, the heavens opened up.

Chapter Two

For dinner that evening, Cassie had her maid assist her into a light green muslin dress, which she knew complimented her blond locks, and then to style her hair into a simple chignon. She refused to admit that her sudden wish to look more mature had absolutely *nothing* to do with Lord Gregory.

Cassie arrived in the parlor before everyone else, so she walked over to one of the windows. She pulled back the heavy draperies and stared outside. Already the ground was covered with a blanket of white, while large snowflakes continued to fall with no sign of letting up. It was amazing to think that just a few hours earlier, they had been enjoying some relatively mild weather. At least they had pleased Cook, for her face had lit up when they'd offered their bounty of fish to her.

"What a difference a day makes."

Cassie turned a wry smile on Gregory, who had just entered the room. He came to stand at another window near her to look out at the winter scene beyond.

"Well, it *is* December," she noted dryly.

"Indeed," he concurred. "At least we didn't decide to wait until tomorrow to go fishing, or else we might have had to cut a hole through ice."

She laughed. "Then we would have had the opportunity to go ice skating," she suggested. "Or even sledding."

He grimaced. "That doesn't sound very warm."

"Perhaps not. But it does sound rather fun." She lifted one shoulder and let it fall nonchalantly. "Either way, I'm sure we'll find something to occupy our time."

He turned to her, his green eyes caressing. "I'm sure we will," he murmured.

Cassie felt that gaze all the way to the tips of her toes. It stirred something inside of her that she had never felt with anyone else.

Thankfully, she was saved by the arrival of her grandmother, with Mr. Pugglesworth held securely in her arms. The dowager sat down with a sigh. "I daresay this cold weather is brutal on an old woman's bones."

Cassie smiled gently as she walked over and joined her grandmother on the settee. She patted her weathered hand. "Is there anything I can get for you?"

Gregory moved to the mantle, where he could be a part of the conversation yet keep his distance as well.

Isabel waved her hand. "It's something we all have to suffer with if we live long enough, I'm afraid." She glanced around the room. "Where is my scamp of a grandson?"

"Right here," Rion said as he strode in. He walked over and kissed the dowager on the cheek. As he straightened, he rubbed his stomach. "Is dinner ready yet? I'm starving."

Cassie knew that if her grandmother carried a cane, that was when she would tap it on the floor. "Don't be impertinent, young man."

11

Instantly, Rion held up his hands and backed away. He walked over and joined Gregory.

As they engaged in their own hushed conversation, Cassie turned her attention back to her grandmother. "How is Mr. Pugglesworth today?"

Isabel looked at the small canine in her lap. "I'm not sure. I think he may be suffering from the same ill affects of this awful weather. He is nearly ten years old, which is quite aged for a dog."

Cassie scratched behind his ear, causing the animal's brown eyes to look at her adoringly. "Oh, I don't know. He'll likely outlive us all."

Isabel smiled. "You may be right."

***

Cassie did her best to ignore Gregory at the dining table, which was rather difficult, considering he was seated directly across from her. Thankfully, Gram was on her left, with Rion on her right, seated at the head, so Cassie concentrated on sneaking some of her food to Mr. Pugglesworth where he snuggled on the floor next to Isabel's chair.

"Now that the snow has finally made an appearance," Isabel spoke up. "I'd like to decorate this stuffy old pile of stones with some holiday spirit."

"Do we really need to drag a bunch of evergreen in here when it's just the four of us?" Rion asked dryly.

"But it won't be for much longer," Isabel countered. "I'm hosting something of a house party until Twelfth Night."

Rion groaned. "Don't tell me I'm going to have to deal with Cousin Agnes!"

Isabel eyed him critically. "And what has she ever done to cause you trouble?"

"She follows me around all doe-eyed." He looked to

Gregory and shuddered.

"It was simply a childhood infatuation," his grandmother sniffed. "Besides, you haven't seen her in two years."

Rion rolled his eyes, but he didn't comment further. Instead, he said, "At least her brother Charlie might be with her, so there could be hope yet."

"Be that as it may," Isabel said firmly, "they are already on their way, along with several of my other nieces, nephews, and grandchildren, and you will do your best to be hospitable to *all* of our guests. Is that clear, Orion?"

Cassie noticed the muscle in Rion's jaw was ticking, although he said, "Yes, Gram."

"Since that is all settled..." Isabel rose. "I believe I will retire for the evening." She spoke down toward her dog. "Come on Mr. Pugglesworth. After everything my granddaughter fed you from her plate this evening, you shouldn't have need of any further scraps from the kitchens."

The pug tucked his tail between his legs rather guiltily, but obediently followed.

As soon as Isabel was gone, Rion stood and threw his napkin down on his plate. "I need a drink," he muttered, and headed for the sideboard. He held up a decanter of sherry. "Who's in the mood for some spirits?" he asked with a mischievous grin.

"Orion Douglas William Matthew Justin Ashcroft!" Cassie gasped. "You're only seventeen! That's far too young to drink spirits!"

"I'm an earl." He snorted, as if that was all the approval he required. "Even if some people around here tend to forget that fact." With that, he poured two fingers' worth of the amber-colored wine and tossed it back in one swallow. "Ah."

Cassie marched over to him and snatched the decanter

off of the sideboard. "That will be enough," she snapped.

"Give it back!" Rion demanded.

She lifted her chin. "No."

"Cassie," Rion said tightly, "you are my sister and I love you, but so help me…"

Gregory held out his hand to Cassie. "Perhaps I might be allowed to intercede?"

She thrust the liquor into his grasp, and he proceeded to take a deep swallow directly from the decanter. "Lord Gregory!" she hissed.

He gave a brief nod, and then handed the bottle back to Rion. "It's not bad." When Cassie sent him a glare that would have murdered anyone else, he stopped her with a whispered entreaty. "Leave him be."

"What kind of an example do you think you're setting?" She turned to face him, at the same time doing her best to ignore the slight shivers that crawled up her spine at Gregory's nearness. Not only did his breath smell slightly of the sherry he'd just drank, but it also carried the decided scent of peppermint. It was an unlikely but rather heady combination.

"Trust me," Gregory said gently. "You have no idea what Rion—" He abruptly broke off what he'd been about to say.

Cassie instantly stilled. "What is it?"

"Nothing." The word was clipped as he moved away, and she knew that any hope of gaining more information from him would be in vain.

Cassie looked between Lord Gregory and her brother. Sighing, she made a decision. She just hoped it was the right one. "Pour me a glass, won't you?"

Rion grinned broadly, but it was the glint in Lord Gregory's eyes that caused her pulse to falter.

***

"Oh, I daresay…" Cassie blinked at the bottom of her empty glass. A small hiccup dared to escape, followed by a decided giggle. "It's all gone."

"You need another!" Rion declared proudly, but when he went to the sideboard to pour some more of the sherry, albeit a bit unsteadily, he closed an eye and frowned at the bottom of the empty decanter. "Blast."

"Personally," Gregory noted dryly as he sat across from Cassie. "I don't think either of you can handle your liquor." He had adopted a casual pose, his hands crossed over his flat midsection, a permanent smirk on his lips.

"Shpeak for yourshelf," Rion returned. "I'm perfectwy fine." However, as soon as the words were spoken, he stumbled and fell to the floor, failing to make it back to the settee.

"I can see that," his friend murmured.

"I'm just going to lie here a bit…" Rion's words trailed off as he closed his eyes. Moments later, a decided snore drifted from his open mouth.

"Oh, dear." Cassie nudged her brother's leg with the toe of her slipper. "I fear he has passed out." She glanced at Gregory. "However shall we get him to his room?"

"I'll take care of him." He tilted his head to the side. "The question is how are you going to get to *your* room?"

Cassie rolled her eyes, but then regretted the action as the room spun. "I shall walk, of course."

Gregory waved a hand. "Be my guest."

She was determined to prove her point, so she stood up as if nothing was wrong. Unfortunately, her feet weren't quite ready to obey her brain, and she fell—right on top of Lord Gregory.

"Ompfh."

"Oh!"

Their responses sounded at the same moment, but awareness soon replaced any shock or embarrassment. As Cassie sprawled across Gregory's lap, she could feel the hard planes of his muscular body, her soft curves pressed against that firm chest, her hands clutching his broad shoulders while his strong hands held onto her waist.

But it wasn't until she lifted her face, finding his only inches away from hers, did she cease to breathe entirely. Almost without conscious thought, her gaze fell to his sculpted mouth. She licked her lips, suddenly wondering what it might be like to kiss him. She felt his hands tighten around her.

"Cassie, don't."

Instead of pulling away she drew closer, bringing her lips perilously near to his. "Why not?" she whispered in a sultry voice that didn't sound like her own.

She thought she heard him utter a curse before he said evenly, "Because you don't know what you're doing, and because I won't take advantage of a woman who has imbibed too much." His gaze, while steady, warmed her from the inside out.

"Are you sure about that?" she countered with a sultry lilt to her voice.

He closed his eyes. "Cassie. *Stop.*"

She heard the warning, but she ignored it. Instead, she dared to flaunt convention, and even her own morality. Leaning forward, she brushed her lips against his. She would have never had the courage to do such a thing when she was sober, because not only was this her first kiss, but this was Rion's friend. *Lord Gregory.*

He shifted beneath her and she broke contact, but when she started to move away, he drew her back to him. "Have you ever been kissed before, Lady Cassie?"

Dear Heavens! She must have been terrible if he'd guessed right away!

She shook her head.

His eyes lit up like a pair of emeralds. "Then your first should at least be done properly," he murmured. Instantly, his lips were on hers, the power behind his kiss enough to shake her to her very core.

One thing was very clear.

This was definitely *not* his first kiss.

When she felt the tip of his tongue brush the seam of her lips, it startled her enough that she gasped. He took advantage of her surprise and wound his tongue inside of her mouth, then withdrew and returned. It was like a sort of mating dance, and it burned Cassie up from the inside out. She pressed against him, her hands clutching his lapels.

She thought Gregory groaned, but when he abruptly lifted her and set her beside him, she realized that it was Rion who had made the noise. He was still on the floor in front of them. She had completely forgotten he was even in the room.

She opened her mouth to speak, say something, *anything*, but Gregory held up a hand.

"Please, Cassie. Just go to bed." He didn't even look at her.

She felt the shame of tears burning the back of her eyelids, as she stood and fled up the stairs.

Chapter Three

Cassie felt Rion aptly mirrored her sentiments the next morning at breakfast. After a night of tossing and turning, where the memory of Gregory's embrace had stayed with her long after she'd gone to bed, Cassie had finally given up trying to sleep. Combined with a sour stomach and a pounding headache, she was not fit company.

Rion was just as boorish, for when she pulled out her chair a little too loudly he gripped the sides of his head. "Can you please keep it down?" he gritted through his teeth.

"Someone's grumpy this morning," she muttered.

He lifted a lid to glare at her with a single, blue eye. "I will be in an even more foul disposition if you intentionally try to vex me."

She sighed, but didn't provoke him any further. In truth, she was too focused on her own misery this morning to even try. At least she was given a reprieve, for Gregory or her grandmother had yet to make an appearance.

As if the very thought of him conjured Gregory in the flesh, he chose that moment to walk into the room. He looked entirely too crisp and fresh that morning, his tan breeches hugging his muscular legs, while his white cravat and dark brown jacket molded to his shoulders with precise tailoring. When he walked past her, she caught the scent of that same wonderful, woodsy cologne that he'd been wearing the night before—when she'd practically thrown herself at him.

She resisted a groan, along with the urge to slink farther down in her chair. When Gregory sat down across from her on Rion's right side, she was determined to ignore him.

"Not feeling well this morning?" he said almost too brightly.

At first Cassie thought he had directed the question at her, but then she saw Rion shoot him a dark look out of the corner of her eye.

"Shut your trap, Dawson," her brother growled.

Gregory laughed, his deep baritone causing Cassie to grit her teeth. Not because she detested the sound, but because she suddenly liked it entirely too much. *What was wrong with her? She was supposed to* detest *Lord Gregory!*

"I didn't tell you to drink that entire bottle of sherry," Gregory chided.

Rion muttered something particularly uncharitable, and then, "I wasn't alone, if you recall."

Gregory cleared his throat. "Indeed, not."

Cassie winced inwardly. *Dear God, could he not even bring himself to mention her name?* She felt her face burn in mortification. She stood abruptly. "If you'll excuse me…"

Cassie didn't wait for a reply, just kept her head down as she rushed out of the room. She walked briskly down the hall, intent on putting distance between herself and

Gregory, when she heard the sound of determined footsteps behind her.

"Cassie, wait." He didn't even bother with the formalities.

She closed her eyes, but reluctantly stopped. With a deep breath, she spun around to face the object of her distress. She held up a hand. "Please. Just forget about last evening. It was a mistake. Rest assured, it won't happen again."

She turned, assuming that had been what he'd wanted to hear. So it surprised her when he said softly, "I'm sorry you feel that way, because I didn't think of it as a mistake at all. It just...took me off guard." He paused. "And if I'm not too forward to say so, I hope it *does* happen again." Cassie's heart stopped. She slowly faced him once more, expecting to see derision or a mocking glint in those green eyes, but they were completely sincere, with a hint of something darker—perhaps even *wicked*—shining in their depths.

"Good morning," Isabel said brightly as she appeared, effectively breaking the spell. She glanced between them, looking somewhat crestfallen. "Don't tell me you've both eaten?"

Cassie felt as though her throat had suddenly closed up, so she was thankful when Gregory replied, "I haven't, Lady Ashcroft." He held out his arm to her. "Might I escort you into the dining hall?"

"An offer from a handsome gentleman?" she teased. "How can I refuse?" She turned to Cassie. "Oh, I nearly forgot. I sent a message round to the stable master this morning to make sure the sleigh is prepared for today."

Cassie gave her first genuine smile of the day. "Thank you, Gram."

The older lady inclined her head then departed on Gregory's arm.

**

Cassie was glad she'd worn her fur-lined bonnet, cloak, and muff for their excursion to gather evergreens. For even with a warming brick at her feet, the winter's chill seeped into her bones. The snowfall had made the air particularly damp, even though it was mid-afternoon.

She glanced out at the white winter scene around her and couldn't help but admire the quiet beauty of the sparkling glade. The sun had finally made an appearance, and paired with tiny ice crystals over the landscape, it seemed almost magical. She wished she had a blank canvas, a brush, and some paints with her. It was an inspiring view for a woman who found comfort in painting. Then again, if she allowed her youthful imagination to carry her away, she might even imagine that she was an ice princess from another realm, traveling to meet her handsome forest prince.

She risked a side-glance at Gregory, seated across from her with Rion, and thought that if she wasn't so rational, she might imagine that she'd already found him.

She snorted at the very idea.

Rion had been in conversation with Lord Gregory, but now he turned to her with a frown. "What's so amusing?"

She shrugged, and tried to cover up her blunder with a plausible excuse. "I was just thinking of something Ann said in town the other day." Of course she seldom spoke to the butcher's daughter any more, not after she'd married and moved to the next county.

She shot a glance at Gregory, whose green eyes sparkled, as if he knew exactly what she was thinking.

Instantly, her heart sped up.

"Care to join our wager?"

Cassie blinked at Rion. "Pardon?"

He rolled his eyes, as if she was slightly dimwitted. "I said we should make a wager for whoever gets the most branches. Are you in?"

She crossed her arms. "I suppose that would depend on your terms."

"The loser has to put them all up." He grinned, as if already assured of his victory. "While the winner watches."

"And gloats?" She smirked. She held out her hand to seal the deal. "You're on." She knew those woods like the back of her hand, probably even better than Rion, especially now that he'd been away at school, giving her unfettered access.

Cassie was thinking that it might also be nice to find a few holly berries to add a bit of color. She should have plenty of time *after* she won the bet.

The coachman brought the team to a stop, slowing the sleigh near the edge of the tree line. Rion immediately vaulted out of the seat and disappeared behind a cluster of pine trees.

"He always has been competitive to a fault," Gregory murmured as he jumped down, although he paused to turn and offer a hand to Cassie. Even though they both wore gloves, a rush of awareness passed between them when they touched. Enough that the moment her feet touched solid ground, Gregory released her while her toes curled in her boots. He shoved his hands in his pockets, his gaze turning distant. "I should probably find him, lest he falls over a dead stump and kills himself."

Cassie frowned as he walked off, but she didn't allow herself to contemplate his pensive mood as she went in the opposite direction, where she knew the best trees were located. In no time at all she had her arms full of lovely, scented laurel. She was careful to keep her cloak close to her, so she didn't snag it on any thorn bushes, as she walked further into the brush in search of berries. After a bit of searching, she finally found what she was looking for.

As she reached down to pick some of the red holly, a blood-curdling growl sounded from behind her.

Cassie instantly froze. She didn't dare turn her head to see what was threatening her, afraid that the slightest movement would aggravate the creature even more.

She pressed her lips together as another growl split the silence, this one even closer. She wanted to cry out, but fear kept her immobile. Surely this wasn't how she would die. Her eyes darted about, her ears straining for any sound of footsteps crunching nearby so that she might call on her brother or Lord Gregory for assistance.

"Cassie. Don't move."

She wanted to sob at the familiar sound of Gregory's calm, deep voice. "What is it?" Her voice trembled.

"A fox," he returned evenly. "You have had the misfortune of stumbling near her den. I wouldn't think she should have any kits at this time of year, but they have a habit of being rather territorial, nonetheless."

Cassie closed her eyes, hearing the sound of another growl, although this one seemed to be directed at Gregory, as it wasn't as close as before. Time seemed to stand still as he slowly began to lure the maddened animal away from her, until she could see him out of her peripheral vision. She knew that at any moment, the fox could lunge out and then it could all be over for one of them. Foxes might be much smaller than a bear, but they could be just as vicious when provoked, and especially if they were protecting their home. Or if they were rabid.

"When I tell you to," Gregory said quietly, so as not to antagonize the fox even further, "I want you to run."

"What about you?" she whispered nervously.

"Just do what I say, Cassie. I'll be fine."

She knew that tone. He wouldn't be dissuaded from his purpose. She just prayed they both got out of the precarious situation in one piece.

She could see Gregory clearly now. He had slowly

made his way around the brush in front of her. She caught a glimpse of his strong, steady form before he threw something at the fox and yelled, "Now!"

Cassie lifted her skirts and fled in the opposite direction. She ran as if her life depended on it and tried to drown out the sounds of a scuffle behind her. Tears streamed down her face as she broke out into the clearing, but even then, she didn't stop until Rion stepped in her path. The scream that had been threatening, ever since she heard that first growl, now burst free.

"What the devil is wrong with you?" her brother demanded.

"There was a…fox…Gregory is…in there…" She pointed back the way she came and managed to stammer out enough of her problem that Rion understood. He walked back to the sleigh and took a rifle from under the coachman's seat. Rion checked to make sure the weapon was primed.

"Don't kill it!" Cassie gasped.

Rion merely grumbled something under his breath about women and their tender sensibilities as he walked away.

Cassie paced back and forth in front of the sleigh. After the third pass, she realized she still clutched the greenery. She quickly deposited it in the back of the sleigh before resuming her anxious walk. The coachman returned with his branches, and she told him what had happened. He was about to go offer his assistance when Cassie finally spied Rion's dark head. The relief that flooded her was instantaneous, especially when Gregory's lighter head came into view.

"Thank God!" She rushed over, looking her brother over from head to toe, breathing a sigh of relief when she realized he was free of harm. However, the moment she turned to Gregory, she saw the blood staining the arm of his jacket. "You're hurt!"

He clenched his jaw. "It's just a scratch."

Of course he would try to brush off the injury as nothing. She marched forward. "I'll be the judge of that. Take off your jacket."

"Cass, it's freezing out here," Rion said. " At least leave the poor man alone until we're back at Ashcroft Hall." He rolled his eyes at Gregory. "All because you didn't want me to shoot the damn thing."

As the coachman climbed back into the driver's seat, Cassie turned to Gregory. "What is he talking about?" The blood abruptly drained from her face, leaving her somewhat lightheaded. "You were attacked because I asked Rion not to shoot the fox?"

He winced as he climbed into the sleigh, where she quickly scrambled in behind him. "I would hate to disappoint a lady."

His tenderness touched her heart, although she chided gently, "I didn't want it spared at your expense."

He shrugged nonchalantly, although she noticed he kept his arm close to his chest. "I'll live."

She lifted a brow. "As long as infection doesn't set in." She called out to their driver, "To Ashcroft Hall immediately!"

"Of course, my lady." He nodded somberly, appearing equally concerned by the turn of events. The sleigh lurched forward.

When she turned back to Gregory, he was grinning unrepentantly, the action setting her pulse to fluttering. "If I didn't know better," he murmured. "I would think you cared what happened to me."

Cassie harrumphed and ignored his statement. "It would serve you right if you lost your arm to gangrene for being so foolish."

He leaned his head back against the seat and closed his eyes, although a lingering smile still touched his mouth. "If I do, at least I can rest knowing that I have your undying gratitude for sparing that creature's life."

***

The moment they walked in the door of Ashcroft Hall, Cassie began issuing orders to the butler. "Lord Gregory has been injured. Please see that hot water, bandages, and a poultice are immediately prepared. We shall be in the front parlor."

"Of course, my lady." Evans bowed.

Cassie went over to Gregory and put his uninjured left arm over her shoulders. He merely lifted his brow. "My arm is hurt, Lady Cassie, not my legs. I'm more than capable of walking on my own."

"Just be quiet," she said. "And let me help you."

When he fell silent, merely tightened his grip on her shoulders, she led him to the settee in the parlor. Once he was seated, she helped him remove his jacket.

Rion plopped down in a chair across from them. "There's no need for all this fuss, Cassie. Gregory is fine. He's had worse injuries than this."

"Perhaps." Gregory's voice was husky. "But I've never had quite so lovely a nurse." He might have been speaking to Rion, but his green eyes caressed her face.

Heat seeped into Cassie's cheeks. Thankfully, two of the housemaids appeared with the requested materials, saving her from any further embarrassment. They set a bowl of steaming water on a side table, along with a towel and several strips of linen. "Cook said this should take care of any issues that might arise from an animal bite."

"Thank you." Cassie nodded, dismissing the maids and getting to work. She wet one of the strips of cloth and turned to find Gregory's muscular forearm was completely exposed. He'd rolled up his right shirtsleeve so she could tend to his injuries, but the sight of that naked bit of flesh caused her to hesitate. Even though there were a few scratches and splotches of dried blood on the golden tanned skin, she was drawn to the faint dusting of light brown hair and the muscles that bunched with the slightest movement. It took her brother a brief clearing of his throat to spur her back into motion.

She had to admit that the wound wasn't as bad as she might have originally thought, but nevertheless, the moment her fingers touched Gregory, a slight hiss escaped his mouth. She glanced at him. "Did that hurt?"

His eyes were almost glowing. "No."

Cassie ducked her head and concentrated on her task. She didn't look at Gregory again until she was finished, and only then it was to murmur something rather unnecessary. "I believe you'll make a full recovery."

"Well, I would think so," Rion grumbled.

They both ignored him as Gregory rubbed his thumb over her hand. "Thank you."

Cassie nodded, not trusting herself to say anything else.

"I guess our wager is void since, in the midst of all the excitement, neither one of us knows who gathered the most evergreen." Rion crossed his arms in irritation. "Then again, all Gregory found was some boring mistletoe."

Cassie risked a glance at Gregory, only to find that his focus was on her mouth.

She sucked in a breath.

Boring mistletoe, indeed.

"I got it!" Rion snapped his fingers, finally drawing their attention. "I propose a game of whist so that we still might determine a winner."

Lord Gregory rose to his feet. "If it's all the same to you, I'll leave you two alone to fight this round together." With a brief bow in Cassie's direction, Gregory left.

She tried to tell herself that she was thankful for his departure because it gave her some private time with her brother. But as his footsteps receded down the hall, she couldn't help but feel a pang of regret.

Chapter Four

That night at dinner, Isabel praised Cassie and Rion's efforts, saying the house was starting to look and smell more like the holidays. After their game of whist, where they declared it another draw, Rion finally conceded defeat and helped Cassie decorate. They wound evergreen boughs around the banister railings and put together a wreath for the front door, and two more over the parlor and dining room fireplaces, nestling the holly berries she had collected throughout the greenery.

While Isabel was pleased, she did not go without expressing regret that Lord Gregory had suffered such an unsavory encounter with one of the local woodland creatures. "I do hope this terrible happenstance won't keep you away from Ashcroft Hall next time," she said to him.

Gregory merely smiled. "I should think it would take more than some discordant fox to deter such gracious hospitality, my lady."

As they continued to converse, Cassie pushed her peas around her plate and couldn't help but wonder if there actually *would* be a next time. Gregory was twenty years old and a future baron. At some point, he would start his own family and drift away from them. It was just the nature of things, so there was no use pretending that it wouldn't happen eventually.

"You're rather quiet this evening, Cassie."

Cassie's head snapped up at her grandmother's commanding voice. "I'm sorry. I guess I'm just tired."

"It sounds as if you all had a rather exciting day," she agreed. "But tomorrow is Christmas Eve, so I fear I must rely upon your goodwill again. I shall need you to take the coach into town. I was notified today that some things I ordered for the house party are ready to be picked up."

"Of course," Cassie said dutifully.

Later, when her grandmother retired, Cassie excused herself. She felt Gregory's gaze on her when she left, but she didn't linger.

In her chamber, Cassie picked up her sorely neglected novel, *Malvina,* by Sophie Ristaud Cottin, and tried to concentrate on the words on the page. Normally, reading was an escape. She could fantasize about other people's lives and dream about what it might be like to live in that certain time or place. That night, it failed to hold her interest.

Instead, Gregory was at the forefront of her mind.

She reluctantly set the volume aside after she scanned the same sentence more than three times. Perhaps she merely needed another selection. Surely something about botany or physics would be enough to put her to sleep if fiction wasn't enough to hold her attention.

Thus decided, she stood and tied her robe about her nightdress. She glanced at the clock on her mantle and saw that it was nearly one o'clock. Were Gregory and Rion still up? She bit her lip, considering the possibility. Even if they were, the parlor and the study were both located at the front of the house while the library was in the rear. If luck was on her side, she could be downstairs and back in her room without anyone realizing she'd even left.

She opened her door and cautiously peered out into the hall. Her long braid swung over her shoulder as she leaned forward. The way appeared to be deserted, so she tiptoed on bare feet to the first floor. She paused and listened intently, but no sound met her ears save for the distant echo of a ticking clock and the slight creak of a settling foundation.

She exhaled a breath and continued on. The library door was slightly ajar, but that was nothing new. One of the servants could have easily left it open. She quietly walked inside and shut the door behind her.

After her eyes adjusted to the darkened room, the only light coming through the window from the moon shining on the snow-covered ground, she walked over to a nearby end table where a candle sat in a holder. She was just about to light the single taper when she heard a soft snore behind her.

Instantly, her chest seized as she slowly turned, where she froze in fascination.

Gregory was sprawled across the upholstered settee, his large frame nearly dwarfing the piece of furniture. He had removed his shoes, waistcoat, and cravat at some point, but he still wore his trousers and shirt, although the sleeves were rolled up to his elbows. The bandage she had made for him was still firmly in place on his right forearm, but that wasn't what dared her to draw closer.

His masculine form had intrigued her earlier, but as he was unaware of her appraisal now, she could look her fill.

She ignored the inner warning that said her endeavor might not end well, should he wake up and find her there, and took another step closer. And another. Until she finally stood directly above him.

He had one arm thrown back behind his head, the other placed across his chest, while a book lay upside down on the floor, its pages in disarray. Instantly, her heart jumped behind her breast. He'd fallen asleep while reading.

Was there anything sexier than a handsome man who read?

She swallowed as she took in his serene face. There was no frown present, as if he was content, even in his dreams. Her gaze dipped lower to the triangle of skin exposed from his open shirt, where a few golden hairs made an appearance on that hard chest. Even his hand was perfectly defined, from the strong fingers and clear-cut veins. She dared to venture farther, past the flat plane of his stomach and his hips—her eyes widening at the slight bulge in his trousers. Her heart beat faster as she continued down past tight thigh muscles and long legs.

As she moved her gaze slowly back up, her gaze resting once more on the area of his concealed manhood, she gasped when she reached his face—for those green eyes were staring directly at her.

***

Gregory didn't know how long Cassie had been looking him over like a prized stud, but considering that his cock was starting to stir with interest, combined with the heightened color on her cheeks, it must have been longer than a few moments.

However, the instant her gaze fastened on his and recognition dawned, her cheeks flamed guiltily as she stumbled backward. Regrettably, an end table impeded her escape when she turned to flee.

As her shin came in contact with the hard wood, she let out a howl of pain. She hopped on one foot, while trying to rub the injured appendage, only to stub her opposite toe on the same offending piece of furniture, after which she promptly fell onto her exquisite bottom.

Gregory might have thought what transpired was rather entertaining if it wasn't for the sheer mortification blossoming on her face.

He rose to a sitting position. "Cassie?" he said softly.

She covered her face with her hands, emotion clouding her voice. "Please, just don't say anything. I couldn't bear it if you made fun of me right now."

"I'm not that cruel, Cassie," he chided gently, as he dared to move closer to her. He lit a nearby lamp, and then squatted on the floor beside her. "Let me see your leg to make sure you didn't break anything."

She moaned. "It felt like it."

This time he couldn't contain a small smile, because he knew that annoying pain all too well. With easy hands, he lifted the hem of her night rail enough to access the damage. Doing his best to ignore the rather lovely shape of her calves and her slim ankles, he searched for an injury. He grimaced at the slight knot forming in the middle of her shin, the area around it already starting to bruise.

He lowered the material before he was tempted to kiss away the pain. "Now for your toe."

His lips lifted again when she slowly slid her left foot over to him. He held her dainty foot in his palm while he asked her to wiggle her toes. As he inspected each one, he said, "I don't think anything is broken, although your little toe has a crack in the nail." When he released her, he let his arms rest on his knees, and murmured, "You might be sore tomorrow, but you'll live."

She reluctantly parted her fingers and looked at him through the gap. "I don't remember ever being so clumsy."

He shrugged. "I have that effect on most women." He was careful to keep his expression completely serious.

Her hands dropped as she punched his arm with her fist, causing him to loose his balance and fall backward onto his rump. "That's *not* funny!" she snapped.

"I'm not laughing, am I?" Although he was.

"Cretin," she grumbled, but her lips began to twitch.

When she made a move to rise to her feet, he slid an arm under her knees.

"What are you—?" She started to protest.

"I have to earn your forgiveness somehow." He winked. "Hang on." With his other arm around her back, he easily lifted her into the cradle of his arms. She instantly wound her arms around his neck. It was a welcome sensation.

He walked toward the door, and her eyes widened in alarm. "What are you doing?"

"Taking you back to your room." He strode out into the deserted hallway.

"What if we're seen?" she hissed.

"Then I'll tell whoever it is that you hurt yourself because you were ogling me and got flustered by my overwhelming manliness."

Her mouth gaped. "You wouldn't dare!" she sputtered, as her cheeks colored delightfully. "And I most certainly wasn't doing any such thing!"

He grinned unabashedly.

Her blue eyes narrowed. "I hope you know that I don't like you at all."

"I know." With that, he kissed her swiftly on the lips, effectively silencing her the rest of the way upstairs.

***

"Glad you could finally join us, Your Majesty," Rion drawled as Cassie finally made an appearance downstairs later the next morning.

She calmly accepted her wrap from the butler, taking her time as she replied sweetly, "I didn't realize you couldn't function properly without my presence." A snort was his only reply, so she added, "For your information, I skipped breakfast because I wasn't feeling well."

In truth, her leg had been throbbing when she woke up. So instead of going down to breakfast, she'd had a tray brought to her room, while her ladies' maid applied a poultice to her shin to help reduce the nasty bruise that had appeared. If her brother thought she was a slugabed, then that was fine with her. It was less mortifying than the truth, that she has been too embarrassed to face Gregory in person.

He eyed her warily. "Are you sure you should be going to the village with us?"

"I'm fine now," she said tightly, wondering if that were actually true.

Gregory walked out of the study, pulling his gloves on as he joined them. "How about you stop antagonizing your sister with questions and let's head out?" He nodded politely at her, as if nothing were amiss, as if she hadn't lost part of her dignity in that library last night. "Lady Cassie."

"Lord Gregory." She inclined her head, and heat swamped her cheeks. Perhaps she wasn't quite as composed as she'd told herself she was.

The trio piled into the coach, which Isabel had ordered brought around earlier. Thankfully, Rion carried most of the conversation, with Gregory offering a nod or a brief murmur now and then, while Cassie stared out the window and tried to ignore the fact that those green eyes focused on her with unsettling frequency. She might not be able to see his gaze, but she could feel it burning through her skin.

She took a steadying breath. She had already been on edge that morning, because every time she'd closed her eyes last night, she felt those strong arms around her, holding her close to that solid, warm chest as he'd gently deposited her at her bedchamber door. She remembered the feeling of loss when he'd released her, the split second of hesitation where she'd thought he might kiss her again, right as he'd bowed and taken his leave. Even now, her nerves thrummed with the anticipation.

"Are you coming with us, or do you plan on sitting in the coach the entire time?"

Cassie glared at her brother before her face heated with the realization that they had indeed already reached the village, and she'd been too busy daydreaming about Lord Gregory to notice.

She stepped down to the ground without a word, ignoring Rion's smirk. With her head held high, she set out for the chandler's shop to pick up the supplies that her grandmother had ordered. After that, perhaps she might pop into her favorite bakery and enjoy a scone and some afternoon tea. While the air was still brisk and the snow crunched beneath her feet, at least the sun had finally made an appearance.

"Mind if I join you?"

When Gregory appeared at her elbow, his presence was so unexpected that Cassie nearly jumped. She assumed he had chosen to take off after her scamp of a brother, and take in the delights of the local pub, or more precisely, the flirtatious serving maids who worked there. "Surely you have better things to do with your time than escort me about."

As if reading her thoughts, he said, "I have no desire to try and beat Rion at the game of coquetry."

"Afraid you'll loose?" She smirked.

His eyes warmed. "What do you think?"

Cassie swallowed as she quickly looked away from that simmering green gaze. Something told her Lord Gregory would win that bet hands down. While Rion had the gift of smooth charm, Gregory's approach was more subtle, almost *lethal* in nature. He would be the type to seduce a woman without her knowledge.

But in the end, she would be glad he had.

Once Cassie had entered the chandler's shop and paid for her grandmother's things, making sure the packaged items would be sent to the coach where their driver would take care of them, she walked back outside. Gregory was still waiting for her. She glanced sideways at him. He was obviously serious in his determination to be her shadow for the day. But just as she was about to speak to him, another voice interceded.

"Can I interest you in a new scarf, my lady?"

Cassie glanced up at the slightly stooped man in front of her. He might have been as tall as Gregory if the full pack on his back hadn't weighed him down. With graying hair and rather ragged brown clothes, he looked at her with a hopeful expression.

"He's just a passing peddler out to take you for whatever you possess," Gregory murmured near her ear. He took her arm, prepared to remove her from the stranger's path, but she dug in her heels.

"I think I shall take a moment to look at what this man has to offer," she said stubbornly. "It would be nice to get Gram something special for Christmas."

She could tell that Gregory wanted to argue with her by the firm set of his jaw, but he merely dropped his hand and moved away to lean against the wall of the storefront they'd just departed.

Cassie grinned at that small victory as she turned back to the stranger. "You said something about a scarf?" she prompted.

A wide, gap-toothed grin spread across his weathered face. He slid the pack off his back and set it on the sidewalk. As he began to riffle through his treasures, his voice instantly changed into that of a born salesman. "Oh, I do, indeed, my lady! My wife is the one who crochets them, and I guarantee you won't find anyone to equal her talents! Not even the seamstresses in Londontown can do such good work…"

Cassie nodded as he continued to ramble on. She refused to look back at Gregory, even though she could have sworn she heard a condescending snort from behind her.

However, it wasn't until the man pulled a pitiful-looking white wool monstrosity from his pack did Cassie actually cringe, although she did her best to keep a polite smile on her face. The man *did* look rather hopeful, after all.

"Here it is! My dear Matilda is a craftswoman, is she not?"

"Indeed." It was all the praise she could manage. Her grandmother would be rather horrified at such a gift, but perhaps Mr. Pugglesworth would enjoy it. She cleared her throat lightly. "How much?"

The older man studied her for a moment, then he said, "You seem like a sweet girl, so I'm going to give you a deal today. Only two shillings."

Cassie definitely heard a choked sputter coming from Gregory this time, although she quickly fished out the requested sum from her reticule. "Thank you, sir."

He bit one of the silver coins before putting them in his jacket pocket. With a wide grin, he handed over the scarf. "I hope your grandmother is most pleased."

She merely nodded as she took the item. He picked up his pack and began to whistle a jaunty tune as he walked off down the street, not nearly as pitiful as he'd appeared only moments before.

She sighed heavily as Gregory finally joined her once more. "I can't wait to see the dowager's face—"

Cassie rolled up the scarf and shoved it under her cloak as she marched across the street, completely ignoring him.

Gregory fell into step beside her, his hands shoved in his pockets. "I suppose you should be grateful that he didn't offer you butter made with candle grease..." he mused.

"Oh, do shut up," Cassie snapped, her patience

coming to an end.

He lifted his brows. "You're not even going to let me gloat for just a little bit?" he asked, a twinkle of merriment in those green depths.

She glared at him. "No." She lifted her chin defiantly, and quickened her pace, although his deep chuckle followed in her wake.

***

At the baker's, Cassie ordered a cup of hot tea and a buttered scone. Before she could pay for the items, Gregory handed over a guinea to the man behind the counter, whose eyes widened perceptibly.

"That's not necessary," Cassie said.

"It's the least I can do, considering I allowed you to be fleeced by that merchant today." Gregory glanced at the wool peeking from beneath her cloak, and drawled, "*Literally.*"

With a huff, she gathered her cloak around her, snatched her things off the counter, and stalked over to a small table and sat down without offering him the courtesy of a thank you. When he joined her a few moments later with a cup of his own tea, she refused to look at him, merely nibbled on her scone.

Several moments passed until he gave a heavy sigh. "I'm sorry, Cassie. I shouldn't have teased you when you were only doing what you thought was right. Helping someone in need is never the wrong course of action."

She finally turned her gaze on him, as if trying to decide if he was being sincere or not, and slowly set down her pastry. "Apology accepted."

Gregory grinned in that heart-stopping way that caused her pulse to hammer in her veins, although he said nothing, just took a sip from his tea.

She took the break in conversation to glance out the

window. She finished off her scone and noted, "It's starting to snow again."

"Indeed it is," he murmured.

"There's nothing like freshly fallen snow, is there?" she mused, her attention still fixated outside. "Of course, the pitter-patter of rain on the roof is nice, but there is just something comforting about a winter storm that makes you want to curl up by the fire with a blanket and a good book. Don't you agree?"

When Gregory didn't reply, she looked back to him, only to see that his jaw had tightened, his focus intent on her. "You paint a serene picture, Lady Cassie. Unfortunately, I was too busy being taught how to run an estate to pay attention to such things."

Cassie swallowed, her throat suddenly tight. Considering the weight of responsibility that had cloaked her brother after their parent's deaths, she knew the pressure that could be placed on a young heir, even if Gregory hadn't yet inherited the title. "I'm sorry. I spoke out of turn—"

He waved a hand in a dismissive gesture. "Don't get me wrong," he added. "I wasn't a prisoner. I was treated like any other son who is to inherit. But with a hovering governess nearby, no siblings, and not many kids my age to associate with, I just never bothered to stop and enjoy the little things."

"It sounds...lonely," Cassie said softly.

Gregory shrugged. "I got used to the quiet, and it was that self-discipline that made me one of the top students in my class at Eton."

It was in that moment that Cassie realized that, not only did Rion need Gregory's friendship, but Gregory also needed her brother's. "Is that why you come to Ashcroft Hall so often? To escape the silence at home?"

As if the shadows around his eyes were magically wiped away, he looked at her with a mischievous wink.

"Well I certainly don't have to worry about that when I visit."

Cassie only rolled her eyes. She couldn't get annoyed at him when he'd just opened up about his past. It was the first glimpse into his personal life that she'd ever been given.

He drained his tea. "You ready to go?"

She nodded. "Now all we have to do is track down Rion."

His lips twitched, his earlier good humor restored. "That, Lady Cassie, is the true test."

***

As it turned out, finding Rion wasn't the hard part; it was convincing him to return to Ashcroft Hall with them that was the challenge.

"You know I can't return to Ashcroft Hall without you." Gregory's jaw was clenched, a sure sign that he was about to explode, although Rion completely ignored the warning.

The young earl sat in the middle of the pub with a buxom wench on his lap, a pint of ale before him. It was a good thing Gregory had asked Cassie to wait outside while he went in to retrieve her brother, for the sight before him would surely have offended her. Then again, that was the destructive path Rion had set upon for the past three years, ever since Gregory had graduated. It was as if he resented his friend's absence and was determined on doing whatever it took to get revenge for being abandoned. Even though he still had Roarke to rely on, it was Gregory who had been there for him through the worst, the early days of school when Rion refused to let his guard down, to let anyone close enough to care for him.

"A couple of hours isn't going to hurt anyone," Rion drawled, his blue eyes roving over the girl who twirled her fingers seductively through his short, dark hair.

"You know I can't take Lady Cassie home without a proper escort," Gregory said through clenched teeth. "It might damage her good name."

"She'll recover easily enough," Rion said dryly, his attention still on his companion.

Gregory had enough. Friend or no, he wasn't about to stand for this slur against Cassie. He slammed a fist down on the table, causing the wood to shake. "You shouldn't take your sister's reputation so lightly," he growled. "If you were a different man, I might just call you out for such poor consideration on her behalf."

That got Rion's attention. If there was one thing that got under his skin, it was a smear on his honor. He shoved the girl aside and stood to face Gregory. The pub suddenly quieted as Rion stood nose to nose with his adversary. Even though Gregory was older, they were nearly the same height, and the fury boiling in Rion's eyes made him seem much older than seventeen. Gregory could feel the stares on them, the pub's occupants surrounding them and waiting with baited breath for what would happen next.

"Stop it!" Cassie's demand caused Gregory to whip his head around to the door. It was enough of a distraction for Rion to act. He snuck in a strong uppercut that caused Gregory's head to snap backwards.

The warmth of fresh blood trickled from a cut to his lip, but Gregory merely grinned. "Is that all you've got, *boy*?" he sneered, knowing that would go even further to get Rion's hackles up. Gregory retaliated with a sharp jab that caused Rion to grunt in pain when he connected squarely with his left eye. He would likely sport a nice bruise in the morning because of it.

Gregory saw Cassie out of the corner of his eye. She rushed forward, as if to intercede. He didn't take his eyes off of Rion, but held up a hand and barked, "Keep her back!"

When he heard her demands to be released, he knew at least someone in this blasted pub had listened to reason. Now, he just had to get Rion to come back to his senses. Unfortunately, they had played this game more than once. His friend had a lot of pent-up aggression that demanded to be released. Someday, Gregory prayed that he would finally be able to come to terms with the personal demons that coursed through him.

A fist came barreling toward his face, but Gregory was ready this time. He jerked out of the way and the blow glanced off his cheek. "Aren't you ready to give up yet?" Gregory mocked. He knew it would send Rion into a blinding rage, but it would also wear him out quicker.

Until then, the punches kept coming. Rion swung his arms with everything he had, while Gregory blocked most of them without ever landing another one of his own. After several minutes, Rion finally collapsed against the bar with great, heaving breaths—and a wide grin. "Damn me, but I will never understand how you stay so conditioned, Dawson."

Gregory simply shrugged. "I don't exert all my energy on unwarranted anger."

"Point taken, as usual," Rion snorted. He put his arm around Gregory with a friendly pat. "Let's get back to Ashcroft Hall. I'm starving."

Gregory grinned in return, but the moment he looked up and saw Cassie's livid expression, he knew the true battle of the day had only just begun.

Chapter Five

Cassie no longer felt any empathy for Gregory. After that horrid display of manly foolishness she'd just witnessed, Rion didn't even qualify for it. Once the two men holding her back had finally released her, she'd stalked out of the pub and headed for the coach, not even glancing behind her to see if the two idiots followed.

All the way to Ashcroft Hall she sat with her arms crossed, utterly furious. She refused to acknowledge either her brother or Gregory, and when she thought they might speak, she shot them a withering glare of disapproval that instantly had them deciding it was probably best not to talk.

Once they were home, Cassie went inside and shut the door, barely taking enough time to hand over her outerwear to the butler and shove the hideous wool scarf in the back of her wardrobe, before going and knocking on her grandmother's bedchamber door, where she knew she would be taking her afternoon repose.

Once she was bade to enter, Cassie went inside. Isabel

glanced up from where she reclined on the bed; Mr. Pugglesworth curled up on his own pillow beside her. The dowager's brows knit, her keen intuition that something was amiss instantly clicking into place. Then again, she had given birth to thirteen children, so she was familiar with family turmoil. "Oh, dear. This doesn't bode well." She patted the bed beside her, a clear invitation.

Cassie sat down, her anger still evident in the tight way she pursed her lips and the stiff way she held herself. "They were animals, Gram. Utterly ridiculous!"

"Who was, dear?"

Cassie could hardly even say their names, she was still so upset with their behavior. "Lord Gregory and Rion!" she seethed. "They dared to engage in a public display of fisticuffs!"

She waited for her grandmother to explode, the way she nearly had, but she surprised Cassie by waving a hand of dismissal. "Is that all? Cassie, they are young men. Very uncouth until they are at least thirty-five, and perhaps not even then."

Cassie's mouth dropped open. "Don't say that you condone their actions!"

"I daresay it would have been preferable if they would have gone out behind the stables, rather than given a public display in the middle of town, but it is almost expected for males to behave in such a manner."

Cassie clenched her fists in irritation but didn't reply.

Apparently noting Cassie's upset, her grandmother softened her tone. "You know as well as I do that Rion is rather…easy to anger. I know you think it was terrible for him to act in such a fashion, but he needs some sort of outlet to direct that frustration. He hasn't allowed himself to mourn your parents properly, and it's festering inside of him like an open wound."

Cassie swallowed tightly as she finally voiced her concerns. "I feel like I've failed him, Gram." She hardly recognized her voice, it was so full of inner turmoil.

Isabel reached out and drew Cassie to her. As Cassie curled up next to her on the bed, her grandmother ran a comforting hand over her hair. "My dear girl, if you failed him then so have I. You forget that I was also grieving the loss of a child. It didn't matter that I had twelve other grown children. Each one is near and dear to my heart." Cassie could hear the sadness in her voice. "Focused as I was on my own personal suffering, I didn't notice the warning signs that Rion exhibited until it was too late. While you and I allowed ourselves to mourn their passing, he never cried or showed any emotion. I'm not sure he ever has." She sighed. "But only Rion can deal with all his pent-up aggression. Once he lets it go, only then will he truly heal. Someday it will all work out. Just promise me one thing?"

Cassie lifted her head.

Her grandmother smiled gently. "Don't continue to blame yourself. Rion will be a grown man soon enough, and it will be time for him to take responsibility for his actions, personal or otherwise." The pug sitting nearby offered a friendly bark, causing them both to laugh. "See? Even Mr. Pugglesworth agrees with me."

Cassie threw her arms around her grandmother. "I love you," she murmured.

"And I, you."

***

Cassie spent the rest of the afternoon in her personal sanctuary. A glass-enclosed atrium in the west wing that Isabel had converted to an art studio when she found out that Cassie had not only a liking for oils, but also a genuine talent for them. Numerous blank canvases were scattered about the room, along with aprons, brushes, palettes, and so many different colors of paint that it would have likely made Michelangelo or Botticelli green with envy.

She often went there when she wished to be alone. Or to think. She found that the sound of the brush against the canvas was rather soothing, and she certainly had a lot on her mind recently. Guests would be arriving later that evening, when Isabel's house party officially commenced. Another fortnight after that would see Rion back at school—and Lord Gregory's departure. The man had only been here for *two days*, but already he had her at sixes and sevens. Until now, Cassie had always looked at the future baron as nothing more than Rion's irritating friend from Eton, but something had changed between them, *shifted*.

Gregory was suddenly...*more*.

Cassie frowned, since her once lovely landscape now had a stripe of green right through the perfectly blue sky. She supposed that was what she got for woolgathering, instead of paying attention to what she was doing.

She picked up a rag and proceeded to wipe off most of the color, but paused mid-swipe. This particular shade looked terribly like Lord Gregory's eyes...

Stop it! She berated herself as she began scrubbing rather vigorously.

"And here Isabel told me that you claim painting is a relaxing hobby for you."

Gregory's unexpected appearance startled her so much that she jerked her arm, her elbow catching her jug of linseed oil and brushes, causing them all to go crashing to the floor. She glared at him. "It used to be." She threw down her rag and bent to gather up the fallen items and bits of broken clay.

He knelt down beside her. "Let me help."

She noted the cut on his lower lip and the slight discoloration on his right cheek from his earlier brawl with Rion, and snapped irritably, "I think you've done quite enough."

He said nothing, just continued to gather up the

shards. Once they had cleaned up the area, he walked over to her easel and studied her current project. "This is amazing, Cassie. I had no idea you were such a talented artist."

She shrugged, uncomfortable with his praise as well as his presence. "It's just something I enjoy doing."

"You do it very well." He smiled in a friendly manner, and she relaxed her guard slightly.

"Thank you."

He turned back to the landscape starting to come to life. "Is this somewhere you've been before, or just a scene brought forth from your imagination?"

She clasped her hands before her and walked forward, daring to stand beside him. "It's supposed to be the coast of Brighton," she offered. "When Rion and I were children, Gram took us there rather often. There was a particular bathing resort that we were fond of."

"Indeed?" Gregory sounded truly interested. "I've heard of certain seaside towns having such attractions, and even that King George attended one in Weymouth, but I've never been to any."

"You should definitely go sometime," she said, warming up to the conversation. At least this was neutral ground and something she knew a bit about. "I understand most of them have private bathing machines in which to change into your swimming attire in privacy. My bathing gown is a bit of a nuisance. It has weights sewn into the hem for modesty's sake, so that it doesn't drift upward in the water."

"How ingenious," Gregory murmured.

"It is," she agreed. "If not rather cumbersome."

"Did your grandmother enjoy these excursions as well?"

Cassie nodded. "Very much so. Some people claim the saltwater is actually more beneficial to one's constitution than the Roman baths. Because of this, there are people called 'dippers' who specialize in various medical treatments. Gram's doctor suggested that she be fully immersed three times to gain the full effect." She shrugged. "Whether he was right or not remains to be seen. Either way, Gram liked going."

Gregory snorted. "I don't know that I agree with much of what these modern physicians have to say."

Cassie smiled. "I supposed everyone has their own opinion."

"That's true enough," he concurred.

They were silent for a moment, then Cassie said, "I'm worried about Rion." She traced the edge of the canvas. "He's...different than he used to be. He isn't like the carefree boy I once knew." Her gaze flickered to him, then hastily away. "I know that we've grown apart these past few years he's been away at school, but after today, I feel like...I don't him at all anymore."

There was a pause, and then Gregory admitted, "I'm sorry to put it so bluntly, but things aren't going to be like they once were. It's true that Rion has been more...unsettled lately, but he's growing up, becoming a man. His entire mentality is shifting, but that doesn't mean he cares any less for you."

Her eyes lifted to meet his. "Are you sure?"

He started to lift his hand, but he must have decided against the action as he let it drop to his side. "How could anyone *not* love you, Cassie?" he asked huskily.

***

Cassie's blue eyes widened, the air around them instantly sparking to life. Gregory could have kicked himself. *What the hell possessed me to say* that*?*

To cover his blunder, he said, "I'm sorry about today." He shoved his hands in his trouser pockets and stared at the floor beneath him. "We both are."

When he glanced back at her, a light frown touched her brow. "I know." She seemed to be debating with herself over what to say next. What came out of her mouth not only surprised him, but touched something deep inside. "In all honesty, I'm the one who should be apologizing to you. I've been rather unforgiving since your arrival, but I want you to know that I believe you're a good friend to my brother." She visibly swallowed. "And I don't think I ever told you how glad I am that you were able to join us for Christmas."

"Thank you, Lady Cassie." His voice was suspiciously deep as his eyes lingered on her face. "That means a lot."

Silence fell, and the air around them suddenly became charged, vibrated with tension.

He had to clench his fists against the pull surrounding them. It made him want to gather her in his arms and kiss her senseless.

Among other things.

He had to get a grip, but it felt as if every nerve ending was heightened and stretched to the breaking point. He knew it would only take the slightest coercion, and he would be putty in her hands.

He had to work to dislodge his tongue from the roof of his mouth. "I should go."

Of course he didn't move. In the end, all it took was a flick of Cassie's pink tongue moistening her bottom lip and he found himself closing the distance between them.

They both sighed at the first touch of his lips on hers. But when his tongue swept inside her mouth, it became a groan of mutual satisfaction.

And they'd only just begun.

***

Cassie thought that the first night she'd kissed Gregory, she had only imagined the heat coursing through her veins, that she could attribute her lightheadedness to the effects of the sherry. She believed her attraction to him in the library, prior to the rather unfortunate events that followed, was because she was simply curious about another male, even if he was the only one who had ever made her breath come faster.

But now she knew that everything she'd felt around Gregory was real. The blood pounding through her body, the pulse beat at her core, it was all *real*.

He was real.

He pulled back and bent down, nuzzling her neck. "You drive me insane, Cassie," he growled. "Why can't I seem to resist you?"

She had no reply as he returned to her mouth and deepened the kiss. She felt a fluttering deep in her midsection, un unquenchable heat that pooled between her legs, a yearning that caused her to press herself more firmly against the hard length of his body. His hand at her waist instantly tightened, before slowly moving upward.

When he grazed the underside of her breast, her breath hitched. When he moved higher, cupping her fully and rubbing his thumb over her nipple, she ceased breathing entirely. She pushed against his hand. "More," she demanded harshly.

He didn't hesitate, tugging down the side of her gown. He urgently peeled back the layers of her undergarments, to free one of her aching breasts. He bent his head and took her quivering mound into his mouth. Cassie saw stars as he laved her pebbled nipple with his tongue. It was more than just intimate.

It was *intense.*

"Gregory, please…" she begged, all sense and reason fleeing in the face of his wicked assault.

"God, Cassie, you're so beautiful…" He backed her against the wall and ground his hips against hers. Her core pulsed with fiery need, and as he began to move against her, the friction intensified. Something was...building inside of her. She wanted more.

She wanted *him*.

But then Gregory was pulling back from her with a muttered curse.

Cassie reached out for him in confusion, her vision still clouded from desire. It wasn't until she heard her brother's voice calling her name that she realized what a precarious position she had put herself in.

With frantic movements, she quickly put herself to rights and tried to re-pin her hair where it was starting to fall down. But it would take more than a few minutes for the color to leave her cheeks, or her trembling to subside. She just hoped that Rion wouldn't notice her state of dishabille.

"Cassie! There you are. Didn't you hear me—"

Her brother came to an abrupt halt the moment he crossed the threshold. He glanced from her, to Gregory, and then back again. Cassie didn't know what he saw, but considering the way his blue eyes darkened with a decided fury, emphasizing the purple shadow still visible beneath his left eye, she knew it wasn't good.

"Gram was looking for you, Cass," he said tightly. He pinned his friend with a glare. "A word, Gregory?" With that, he turned on his heel and stalked away.

Even though it was obvious Gregory was supposed to follow suit, he paused and turned to Cassie, those green eyes still shimmering with desire. "Cassie..." he began.

She turned away from him, frustrating tears already starting to blur the canvas in her line of vision. "Don't say anything. Just go."

He hesitated a moment longer, and then she heard his footsteps as he departed.

Only then did she allow the tears to fall.

And she didn't even know why she was crying.

Chapter Six

Cassie didn't know what Rion and Gregory might have discussed in private, but she was spared from wondering too long by the appearance of her ladies' maid announcing the arrival of Isabel's long-awaited houseguests. Cassie immediately changed into a clean cornflower blue muslin, and as she went downstairs, she had to blink, for the foyer had filled with so many people that the entire manor was buzzing with activity. The moment she appeared, she was beset by squeals of delight from her female relations. As Cassie greeted everyone in turn, it didn't escape her notice that her brother and Gregory had yet to make an appearance.

Cousin Agnes, Rion's personal arch nemesis, had red hair and sparkling brown eyes. She embraced Cassie in a hug so fierce that she thought a rib might have cracked from the pressure. "It's so lovely to see you again! It's been entirely too long."

She giggled in a manner similar to so many other young debutantes, and Cassie had to bite the inside of her cheek to keep from groaning aloud. Rion might not know it, but she had never particularly cared for the girl either. She thought she was entirely too spoiled and flirtatious, although she said politely, "It's good to see you again, Agnes."

"Don't forget me!" Cousin Phoebe came forward, although she didn't hug Cassie, but kissed the air on either side of her face, her dark curls bouncing. "I hear it's how the French greet each other." She winked, her equally dark eyes dancing.

"Oh, yes, the French ways are completely enthralling. Remember the storming of the Bastille that started the Revolution?" Phoebe's father, Cassie's Uncle Francis remarked dryly.

"Can't you leave politics off the table for one evening?" chided his wife, Aunt Margot. She looked at Cassie with a roll of her eyes. "I daresay ever since Napoleon's coronation this month, he's spoken of little else but the war."

"Mark my words." Her husband sniffed. "This is only the beginning of the emperor's power. Its effects on England…"

His words trailed off as his wife pulled him away.

After that, there was a steady stream of guests, as carriage after carriage pulled up in front of the manor. Cassie had lost count somewhere around twenty-five, but that was likely only half of the occupants filling up the front parlor in anticipation of the evening meal. Most of her grandmother's children and their families were familiar to her, but there were a few new faces since they had last gathered at Ashcroft Hall—for her parents' funeral. Cassie was introduced to new babies, husbands, and wives—and still, Rion and Gregory remained absent.

She considered sneaking away to look for them, but her courage faltered when she contemplated the rather awkward situation she would no doubt place herself in.

It wasn't until the evening meal was called and everyone was seated that they finally strode into the dining hall. At first glance everything appeared normal, but the tight lines around Rion's mouth and the hard glint in Gregory's eyes suggested otherwise. Cassie hated to think that she might have caused discord between them, but neither had she anticipated her unexpected feelings toward Gregory.

What made matters worse was when Agnes immediately noted their bruises. "Still getting into scrapes, I see, Cousin Rion." She clucked her tongue in disapproval.

It only caused Rion to grin. "I forgot how much I *didn't* miss you, dear Agnes."

"That's enough, you two," Isabel scolded lightly as they took their seats.

Cassie was quiet throughout much of the meal, allowing the conversation to drift around her, although Phoebe did her best to engage her when possible. Cassie didn't look at Gregory, although she could feel his gaze on her from time to time.

Along with Rion's.

Once the meal was concluded, most of the older people decided they would retire, claiming that after a day or more of travel they were ready for bed, and that they would like to wake up on Christmas morning fully rested.

Thus Cassie, Gregory, Rion, Agnes, Phoebe, and five of their other cousins, all male and of a similar age, were left behind to entertain themselves. They relocated to the parlor and wandered off to different locations about the room, although Cassie was aware of Gregory's presence above all others, as he stood by the mantle next to Rion.

Of course, with that much male fortitude in one room, someone was bound to come up with a perfect idea for a way to alleviate their boredom.

"Here we go." Agnes was playing cards with Phoebe,

but she rolled her eyes at her brother, Charles, who had made the initial suggestion that now hung in the air.

"Well, it *is* a tradition on Christmas Eve," Jeffrey murmured from where he sat sprawled in a chair, his leg hanging over the side.

"You would take his side," Phoebe protested. "It's foolish."

"Are you scared?" Nicholas teased, a wicked grin on his face.

But it was Agnes who snorted. "Not of you."

"What about you?" Charles gestured to Uncle Jasper and Aunt Suzanna's three sons, who stood in a cluster by the east windows. With their equally light blond hair they looked like a trio of angels. A complete contrast to Nicholas and Jeffrey with their dark coloring, or even Charles with his red hair and freckles. "Care to play a harmless game of Snapdragon?"

Out of the three, Stephen, Marcus, and Frederick, the eldest was the one who spoke. "I agree with Phoebe." Marcus replied. "It's not only foolish, but dangerous to set a bowl of brandy on fire in order to fish out a handful of raisins."

"But whoever gets the most will find their true love within the year!" Agnes cried, as she started to warm up to the idea.

"Don't you have enough of those bucks sniffing about you in London during the Season?" Nicholas snorted.

She glared at him. "That is then. This is now. I want to know if I should choose one over the other."

Marcus shook his head. "Rumor is that you will find your true love, not uncover the identity of whom it might be." He walked toward the door, his brothers in tow. "You'll forgive us if we don't join you. I'd like to wake up tomorrow without the smell of burnt flesh in my nostrils."

"Who needs them?" Jeffrey shrugged as they departed. "They've always been boring, in my opinion. If we're lucky, they'll join the war and come back on a board."

Phoebe gasped. "That is a horrible thing to say!"

Agnes clapped her hands together, her focus now on the game at hand. She turned to Rion and began issuing instructions, as if she were the one who had made the suggestion in the first place. "We shall need a large, shallow bowl…"

Cassie's brother merely groaned, but rose to his feet, for he knew if he didn't he'd never get a moment's rest.

"I suggest that we move back to the dining room," Charles suggested.

"Yes," Nicholas drawled. "We shouldn't want to catch any of the draperies on fire in here."

Cassie winced but followed suit. She risked a single glance behind her to see if Gregory meant to join them, as the only non-blood relation present. With a sigh, he reluctantly pushed off of the mantle.

Once Rion had returned from the kitchens and everything was prepared, the eight of them gathered around the glass bowl filled with brandy and raisins. For a moment, no one spoke, just stared at the seemingly harmless item. At last, Nicholas said, "Let's get this game started." And then he lit the brandy on fire.

At first, the liquid appeared almost unholy, a blue flame flickering across the surface. Cassie felt a sense of trepidation until Agnes turned to her with a smirk. "What are you waiting for?" With that, she shot her hand out and grabbed one of the raisins from the center, the flames appearing to part for her. "One," she announced smugly as she popped it into her mouth.

"My turn." Charles shoved up his sleeve and shoved his hand into the bowl, but yelped when some of the hair on his arm was singed.

"Not so lucky as your sister, eh, Charlie?" Jeffrey chortled.

Charles rubbed his arm. "Let's see you do any better."

"Challenge accepted." Jeffrey quickly grabbed a raisin that was floating on top of the flickering brandy. "One." He chewed with humor-filled eyes.

After that, the bowl was passed around to the others, until it finally stopped before Cassie. She stared at the unholy light, wishing that she'd taken Marcus's advice and bowed out, but since all eyes were on her, she had no choice but to try, or else be considered a coward.

But if she was going to injure herself, she intended to make it count.

She stared at the raisins floating around the bowl. Unlike the others, who quickly dipped their fingers in and tried to only grab one raisin, she intended to put an end to this idiocy once and for all. With a deep breath, Cassie thrust her hand in.

Instantly, the sharp whip of the flame tried to burn her, the warm brandy smothering her hand in heat. The room went silent as she cupped her hand and waved it slowly through the inferno. She had to grit her teeth to keep from tensing at the pain that lanced up her arm, but she refused to give up. Seconds passed, although it felt much longer as she scraped the bottom of the bowl, determined to pluck out every last raisin.

It wasn't until she heard Gregory murmur her name, almost on a plea, that she finally withdrew her hand. The moment the air hit her tender flesh she nearly went to her knees, but she opened her fist and let twelve raisins fall to the table. Not a single one remained in the bowl. "I win."

Seven pairs of eyes looked at her as if she wasn't even human, but it was only Gregory's steady green gaze she saw as Agnes muttered, "And I thought I was competitive. I think she deserves to find her true love after that display."

In answer, Cassie turned and walked away.

She was halfway to the kitchens when she had to stop and cradle her arm against her chest. It burned as surely as if her arm was still smothered in the brandy.

"What the hell were you thinking?" Gregory's voice was hoarse but furious as he came up behind her. He didn't wait for her to reply, but gathered her up in his arms and took her upstairs to her bedchamber. "Stay there," he ordered as he laid her on the bed.

Cassie could only manage a weak nod as he left. She had no intention of going anywhere.

He returned a short time later with strips of linen, a bowl of water, and an ointment he'd procured somewhere. Cassie eyed the foul concoction warily, but said nothing as he laid the items on the side table by the bed, and then pulled over a chair and sat down. He dipped a rag and paused to look at her. "This might hurt."

Cassie closed her eyes. "It can't be any worse than it is now." There was a pause, and then he laid the cloth against her burning skin. She instantly sighed in relief.

It wasn't until he applied the salve and wrapped her arm in the dry strip that he said, "I don't think it's going to scar, but I can guarantee it's going to be sore tomorrow."

She opened her eyes and attempted a smile in an effort to lighten the mood, but it likely came out as more of a grimace. "This is some holiday, wouldn't you agree? First, you get injured by that fox, and then the fight yesterday, and well, I suppose today was my turn."

"Is that why you did it?" he asked harshly. "To prove a point?"

"Not in the manner in which you're thinking." She shrugged. "I only wanted to end that stupid game."

"You didn't have to participate in the first place," he pointed out.

She studied that handsome face just inches from her own. "You did."

"Only because I had the feeling you might do something equally foolish." He shook his head. "Snapdragon has been around for years, but it's pointless. In fact, that's what Rion was ranting to the others when I left."

Again, she tried to summon an appropriate smile. "You don't think I'll find my true love within a year then?"

He stilled. "Do you?"

"Honestly?" She sighed. "I think it's all illusion and deception."

Finally, his mouth kicked up at the corner. "In that case, there may be hope for you yet."

She snorted. "I wish I could say the same for you."

He merely grinned.

While Cassie wanted to keep the mood light, she had to know, "What did Rion say to you today?"

Gregory clenched his jaw. "Nothing you need to worry about."

"What a terribly cryptic answer," she teased.

"It's all you need to know."

He stood, and she knew that was all he was willing to say on the subject. "If your arm starts to bother you, just add more ointment. As long as you keep it moisturized, that should take care of the sting."

She swallowed heavily. "Thank you, Lord Gregory."

He reached down and brushed her cheek with his fingers. "It's my pleasure, Lady Cassie." With that, he quietly let himself out.

***

After Gregory shut Cassie's door, he leaned against it with a sigh, his earlier

conversation with Rion replaying in his mind.

"What the hell do you think you're doing?" Cassie's brother had demanded once they had been out of earshot. He'd pulled Gregory into an abandoned room and shut the door behind them.

Gregory ran a hand through his hair. His body was still thrumming with desire, so while he'd expected no less than a firm reprimand from Rion, he hadn't particularly been in the mood for a squabble. "As if you've never been in a similar situation before."

"Cassie is different," Rion snapped.

"Yes, she is," Gregory shot back. "For *you*."

Rion bunched up his fists, and for a moment, Gregory had thought they might be engaging in another round of fisticuffs. "I'm warning you. Leave her *alone*."

"Or what?" Gregory scoffed, baiting the tiger in his cage. "You'll demand satisfaction? Shall it be pistols or swords at dawn?"

"Don't push me!" Rion snarled, indeed taking another threatening step closer. "Don't forget that you are a guest in *my* house, which means that I should be able to trust you with my sister's virtue!"

Gregory sighed heavily, the fight suddenly leaving him. "You're right, of course. Forgive me." He shook his head. "I honestly don't know what's come over me. Cassie used to irritate the hell out of me, and I know she used to feel the same about me. I...just don't understand when all that changed."

At Gregory's explanation, Rion's fists unclenched, his manner turning less hostile. "I suppose we all have our weaknesses, especially when it comes to a pretty face." He shoved his hands in his pockets. "It's just...hard for me to imagine that Cassie is a woman and not just my sister."

Gregory had certainly been able to sympathize with that. For years, he'd only thought of Cassie as the blond-haired, blue-eyed hellion that lived at Ashcroft Hall, but *now*...

Gregory snapped back to the present with a shake of his head. He supposed he should return to the dining room in case Rion needed any help knocking some sense into his cousins.

Chapter Seven

Christmas morning dawned with a fresh blanket of white. Cassie had received a note earlier from Agnes, asking if she might like to go riding after breakfast, to which she'd agreed. No doubt her cousin was trying to make amends for insisting on that ridiculous game of Snapdragon.

After performing her morning toilette, Cassie had her maid lay out her plum velvet riding habit. Thankfully, the girl didn't ask about her wrapped arm, only inquired if she needed anything. Cassie had declined, for after Gregory's careful ministrations, the burn didn't feel as bad as she thought it might. In truth, it hardly stung at all.

She was the last one to make an appearance downstairs, and her grandmother frowned lightly with disapproval. As usual, Isabel held Mr. Pugglesworth in her arms. "Ah, there you are, Cassiopeia. I had nearly given up on you." She patted the only empty chair next to her. "I saved you a seat."

Cassie grimaced at she sat down beside her at the

table. "*Must* you call me that?" she grumbled.

"It is your name, is it not?" Isabel sniffed in reply.

Cassie sighed heavily. "Unfortunately."

"It's nothing to be ashamed of," Isabel went on. "Your parents named you both according to the alignment of the stars on the night each of you were born."

Charlie, overhearing the dowager's statement, gave a mocking snort. "So, *Orion*, does that mean you are our devoted hunter?"

Rion grinned. "I have my moments, but then, nothing can compare to my dear sister with her *unrivaled* beauty…"

They chortled, while Cassie shot them both a withering glare.

It was Gregory who cleared his throat and murmured, "Do you not agree that Cassie is just as lovely as her namesake claims?"

His softly spoken query hung in the air for several moments, the entire table falling silent, before Uncle Raymond, Nicholas' father, said, "Hear, hear, Lord Gregory! Our dear Cassie is indeed a bewitching young lady who shall set London on its ear next Season."

Isabel huffed beside Cassie. "Raymond, we've talked about this—"

"And I have listened, Mother," he interrupted. "Constance and I—" he gestured to his wife, by his side "—have discussed it at length recently, and we both decided that it's time the gel had the chance to snag a husband. She won't make a good match rusticating in this moldy castle. Besides," his voice grew tight. "It's the least I can do to honor my departed brother's memory."

Isabel was silent for a moment and then she said, "I will consider it."

After that, the conversation shifted to other things, including the upcoming Christmas celebration that evening.

Agnes took that as a good time to slip away. She gestured to Cassie with an anxious wave of her hand. Cassie smiled, but dutifully followed her cousin to the stables where two mares waited, a dappled gray and a chestnut, both already saddled, their bridles held by the stable master, an older gentleman with a shock of white hair. "It's been awhile, my lady."

"Yes, it has," she agreed, offering him a friendly smile.

He bowed politely. "Enjoy your ride."

"Thank you, Stratford."

Once Cassie and Agnes were both atop their mounts, their legs thrown over the saddle horn, they began a gentle walk across the fresh snow. Even now, the gray clouds overhead threatened more. "I forgot how much I missed riding," Cassie sighed, more to herself than to her cousin.

"I should do it every day if I lived in the country," Agnes remarked. "Unfortunately, Mother loves town so I don't always get the opportunity."

Cassie shrugged. "It's not so much fun to ride alone."

Agnes turned to her with a puzzled frown. "Don't you have anyone your age in the village, or even your ladies' maid, that you could ask to accompany you?"

Cassie grimaced. "My ladies' maid detests horses, and most everyone my age in the village is…busy with their own families." As her horse shuffled beneath her, she forced her grip to relax on the reins.

"I…see," Agnes murmured, but Cassie wondered if she truly did.

***

Cassie was quite sure she was frozen through by the time they returned to Ashcroft Hall nearly three hours later. She had never been more relieved to see the gray-stone, Gothic structure with its turrets and towers. The sprawling estate looked intimidating at the best of times, but just knowing that there was a warm fire somewhere inside was enough for her to sigh in relief.

However, the moment they rode into view, the front door opened and Rion, Phoebe, and the rest of the cousins from the night before—the angelic trio and Lord Gregory excluded—came striding down the steps.

"It's about time you returned," Rion said with a wink in Cassie's direction.

"Did you miss us, dear cousin?" Agnes purred as she dismounted, handing over her reins to the waiting groomsman.

Cassie dismounted in an effort to hide a smile as Rion visibly winced. Her humor didn't last long as a perfect ball of snow hit her on the shoulder.

Rion laughed.

"Ow!" Cassie immediately bent down and packed her own retaliating orb, before hurling it right at her brother's chest. It exploded, sending ice crystals flying into his face and coating his hair.

After that, a full-blown war broke out.

Someone shouted *"Run!"* and they all scattered like leaves in the wind. They hid wherever they could block an attack, but still fire a few shots of their own. Behind bushes, the corners of the house, it wasn't long before the front lawn was a volley of flying white balls.

"I can't believe *I* wasn't invited to go riding!" Phoebe shrieked, getting into the spirit of the battle as she attacked Agnes, who had slipped behind a tree.

"Oh, do stop your whining!" Agnes returned, easily ducking her throw, before getting caught in the leg by Nicholas.

He snorted—right before Jeffrey caught him in the face.

"You always were too cocky for your own good," Jeffrey said.

Charlie dared to peek out from the side of the house, having yet to pick a target, before his sister sent two snowballs flying in his direction. "Are you going to participate or not, Charles?" Agnes demanded.

Cassie didn't remember ever having such a splendid time. As she listened to the verbal shots being fired around her, the ones that rivaled the physical ammunition, she tossed a frozen sphere in her hand and waited for the right moment to strike. Patience was key in this game.

She abruptly grinned as a new arrival walked outside.

She'd just found a target.

"Gregory!" Rion warned. "Look out!"

His warning came too late, for Cassie had already thrown back her arm and let it fly. The ball hit him squarely in the side of the head, knocking his hat off, and causing him to stumble backward.

"What the *devil*—" Gregory muttered as he shook his head. It wasn't until his dark blond hair was free of most of the frozen snow coating the strands that he looked up and noticed Cassie's unspoken challenge.

"I do hope that wasn't too...*cold* for you, Lord Gregory." She threw his words back to him from the first night he'd arrived, when he had spoke of his disdain for the winter season.

His lips instantly twitched, and those green eyes flickered with a swirling emotion she wouldn't dare name, as he'd reached down and packed together some fresh snow. "On the contrary, Lady Cassie..."

After that, it became a personal war between the two of them.

She easily dodged his first attempt, as she ducked down behind the hedgerow, but the ones that followed were a bit more difficult to evade. She wondered if it had been such a good idea to unleash the beast within Lord Gregory, for she had never seen anyone throw with such accurate precision. She had to call on several years' worth of battles with Rion in order to outwit him.

Cassie was breathing heavily from her exertions, each exhale fogging in front of her on a white cloud, as her fingers started to grow numb inside her gloves. But fate smiled upon her in the form of another distraction. Marcus and his brothers made the mistake of coming outside— they instantly became the objects of everyone's attentions. Within minutes, their clothing was coated with frosty snow.

"Not today, ladies," Stephen cooed, and Cassie knew that he wasn't just speaking to the women present.

At this point, no one even bothered to try and hide. The battlefield was open while they all faced off against each other.

Cassie had to smile as their laughter filled the yard, but suddenly her merriment died when she realized that Gregory had disappeared. "Blast," she muttered to herself. "Where did he go?"

She was contemplating trying to look for him, when she was struck solidly—right on her backside. She jumped with a yelp of surprise, and turned to glare at Gregory, who had managed to sneak up behind her.

"Direct hit." He stalked her, another snowball at the ready. "Do you concede?"

She lifted her chin, along with her arm which held another snowball. "Never."

Cassie expected Gregory to release his weapon, but instead he caught her around the waist and pulled her flush against him. "I said—Do. You. Concede?"

"*No.*"

"Then you leave me no choice." She thought he might kiss her, had actually *hoped* he would, but instead, he took his snowball and placed it on the back of her neck.

Cassie screeched as the cold snow touched the tip of her spine. "That's not fair!" she cried as she wriggled in his grasp. But then she remembered she was not without her own tricks. She smashed her nearly forgotten palm of snow right on the top of his bare head.

"Do *you* concede?" she asked smugly.

His mouth only kicked up at the corner in a sly grin. "Never." He dropped his voice. "And always."

This time, he did kiss her, and it nearly melted the snow beneath Cassie's feet.

***

Cassie was grateful for the steaming cups of hot chocolate that were ready and waiting for them when they all piled inside. They were cold, wet, and shivering, yet every face was wreathed in smiles.

Cassie took her cup to her room and changed out of her sodden clothes, as did everyone else. She sat by the crackling fire in her robe, hoping that the feeling would return to her limbs soon. She patiently waited while a bath was prepared, then sighed as she sank into the steaming, lilac-scented water. Once she dried off, she wiggled her warm toes in front of the fire as her maid helped her into a light green satin gown with a delicate lace overlay embroidered with green flowers. It was something special Cassie had chosen in honor of this evening, and she thought it fit the spirit of the season perfectly. Thankfully, due to Lord Gregory's miracle ointment, she no longer required a bandage for her arm.

After her hair was styled into an elegant chignon, a sprig of holly berries placed in the midst of the golden curls, she opened her door to go downstairs, but she stopped at the sight of Lord Gregory leaning against the wall opposite her room.

He was wearing a black jacket and trousers, a crisp white cravat and shirt, but it was the emerald waistcoat he wore that caused her pulse to flutter, as it emphasized those green eyes. His bold gaze raked her from head to toe. "I wouldn't mind it if you were my present to unwrap, Lady Cassie."

"You're incorrigible."

His grin was slow to appear, but when it did, it was rather wolfish. "You have yet to learn how deep my depravity truly goes, my dear." He held out an arm to her. "Shall we?"

Cassie wasn't sure if he was teasing her—or if he might just be speaking the truth. Either way, she accepted his offering, and he escorted her downstairs. Rion was the only one present when they entered the parlor. Cassie watched as he poured a healthy draught of port and downed it all in one swallow.

She shook her head. "I don't see how you can stomach anything after all that sherry you consumed the other night."

"*Uses promptos facit.*" He winked before taking another healthy sip.

Cassie turned to Gregory, who translated dryly, "Use makes perfect."

She rolled her eyes, but didn't say anything further, as Agnes entered the room on her brother Charlie's arm. Cassie thought she heard Rion mutter something about "something fortifying" as he downed another glass.

Slowly, the rest of the party began to trickle in. But it wasn't until Isabel finally made an appearance with Mr. Pugglesworth that the butler announced dinner.

Cassie's mouth was almost watering just thinking of the Yorkshire pudding that was on the menu for this evening. In light of all the activity earlier that day, she'd missed lunch.

She sat down at the table, surprised when Gregory sat beside her. He normally took the place to Rion's left as his guest of honor, but after she caught her grandmother's keen eye, she knew the reason for the change. She felt her cheeks warm, especially when Gregory's muscled thigh brushed hers under the table. But he was a perfect gentleman and didn't even tease her, so she started to relax and actually enjoy herself. It turned out Gregory was a rather delightful conversationalist and quite witty as well.

Once everyone's appetites were sated, they returned to the parlor, where everyone scattered about in various locations—standing, sitting, or even relaxing on the floor—the main focus was on the mountain of gifts that had suddenly appeared in the corner.

Within moments, the area was abuzz with activity. A few of the smaller children clapped with open glee at the presents, although the older ones had a special sparkle in their eye when they were handed a package with their name on the tag.

The room was quickly covered with paper and string, as the gifts were torn open amid laughter and enthusiastic cries of happiness.

It was a Christmas that Cassie would surely remember for years to come. Not only because family was present, but because of Lord Gregory. He sat beside her on the settee, his arm thrown across the back, appearing completely at ease as he chatted with Rion on his other side. Someday, when the two of them went their separate ways, she would recall this holiday with a bittersweet memory.

It was the one where she first fell in love.

"Oh, look at this! Dear Cassie bought you something, Mr. Pugglesworth." Isabel nearly preened when she was handed a gift on behalf of her prized pug, turning Cassie's attention back to the present. "Shall we see what it is?" Cassie had finally decided, just that morning, to wrap the wool scarf she'd bought from the peddler, although her pride wouldn't allow her to actually give it to her grandmother.

The dog barked in reply and sniffed the package. Cassie held her breath as Isabel carefully removed the covering.

"Oh...my," Isabel murmured as a small growl emanated from the pug. She cleared her throat and looked at Cassie. "Wherever did you manage to find something so...unique?"

Cassie discreetly elbowed Gregory in the ribs when he dared to snort. "It was a traveling merchant." To try and make it seem more special and less hideous than it was, she added brightly, "He said his wife made it."

"Indeed." Her grandmother smiled. Unfortunately, Mr. Pugglesworth wasn't as forgiving. With another growl, he jumped down from Isabel's lap and reclined by the fire, although he kept a wary eye on the wool in his mistress's possession.

Cassie tried to hold in a laugh, but Isabel must have thought she was disappointed, for her grandmother said kindly, "I'm sure he'll come around, dear."

Cassie merely nodded.

Thirty minutes later, the chaos had simmered to an excited murmur as all the gifts had been handed out. Cassie had done rather well herself, receiving a new bonnet from her grandmother, a pair of hair combs and several pieces of new jewelry from her relations, but her favorite thus far was a miniature of Rion.

When she'd opened her brother's gift, she turned to him with a gasp. He'd only winked and said, "Who *wouldn't* want a picture of me?"

Cassie had merely rolled her eyes at him, but gently wrapped the small portrait back up to be treasured all the same, knowing that the true sentiment behind the gift was genuine.

After the merriment had died down and some of the older family members and smaller children had departed to their bedchambers, Agnes approached Cassie with a brilliant smile. Cassie couldn't help but eye her cousin warily, considering what had happened the day before.

"I've been speaking with some of the other cousins, and we were hoping that you and Rion might take us on an extended tour of the castle."

Rion overheard her suggestion and lifted a dark brow. "Tonight?"

Agnes lifted her chin. "Unless you have something more important to do...?" She glanced around, as if he might find an object of more interest at hand.

He crossed his arms. "What are you up to now?"

Agnes sighed heavily, as if she couldn't fathom why he didn't just go along with her plan. No doubt she was used to getting her way. "Only that it will be fun, and the last time we were here we didn't get to go exploring."

"Hoping for some secret passages, are you?" Rion asked dryly.

"And maybe a dungeon," she returned, almost hopefully.

"Not that I know of," Rion said, although his grin widened. "But if there was, rest assured, that is where *your* rooms would be."

She glared at him. "I can't *believe* we are blood relation," she snapped, and then promptly stomped off.

"Rion." Cassie gave a long-suffering sigh. "*Must* you always tease her?"

He snorted. "It's not my fault she makes it so easy." He turned to Gregory. "What about you? You already know this castle nearly as well as I do. Are you going to partake in another frivolous event with my annoying cousins, or have you had your fill?"

Gregory turned his warm gaze on Cassie. "I say let the games begin."

***

Of course, Rion was right. After his numerous visits to Ashcroft Hall over the years, Gregory knew every single turret and battlement. As far as secret passages, the manor *did* have a few, although he wasn't sure if Cassie even knew where they all were. Rion claimed that she'd always wanted to know, but that he'd never told her, enjoying the fact that he had a bit of knowledge he could hold over her head.

No, Gregory's desire wasn't to reexamine everything the castle had to offer. He just wanted to spend some time alone with Cassie. He hadn't forgotten the taste of her lips on his, and the memory of that torrid embrace in her art room was burned on his brain indefinitely. He had been restless for more ever since.

If he could manage to distance them away from the others, for just a brief time...

He might be able to tell her how he truly felt.

Or, at least, have the opportunity to properly *show* her.

With that in mind, he realized he was rather eager to begin exploring.

But it wasn't the castle he was looking forward to investigating.

Chapter Eight

After Rion had agreed to host them on an in-depth tour of the manor, Agnes approached the rest of the cousins and told them that whoever wished to take part should reconvene in the library at midnight, and those who declined could remain in their rooms like the dullards they were.

Everyone thought the angelic trio would bow out, but to the surprise of the rest, Stephen, Frederick, and Marcus all strolled into the room, just as the clock on the mantle chimed the twelve o'clock hour.

"As if we could let you wander about this drafty stone manor without proper supervision," Marcus drawled by way of an explanation.

"We're not the ones who need overseeing," Nicholas noted dryly. "You are the ones who can't manage to leave each other's side for more than an hour at a time." He lifted a sardonic brow. "Tell me, do you bathe together as well?"

Stephen only smiled. "There is strength in numbers,

cousin."

Phoebe rolled her eyes and said irritably, "Are you quite finished? If so, then perhaps we might do what we all came here to do?"

She marched out into the hall with Agnes and her brother, Charlie trailing behind.

Jeffrey shrugged and followed suit, leading the way for the rest to trickle out.

Rion stood apart from the rest as the lead, and turned to face the assembled group. "Do you want the sordid history, how our ancestors conquered the Romans hundreds of years ago, or do you just want to see the really macabre stuff?"

"Macabre, please," Agnes said sweetly.

The rest of the vote was equally unanimous.

Rion snorted as if he wasn't at all surprised. "Very well. Follow me." With that, he turned on his heel, while everyone else remained close behind.

Except for Cassie and Gregory.

Cassie bit her lip. This was her chance to finally find a few moments with him all to herself. "Oh!" She paused at the threshold, making a show of acting as though she were injured, adding a slight limp for effect. Her ploy worked, for Gregory fell back, looking at her distressed face with concern. The rest of the party didn't seem to notice their absence, for they turned a corner, their hushed voices fading. "What seems to be the matter?"

"I don't know. A pain just shot up my leg." Cassie bent down to make a show of rubbing her shin. She glanced up at Gregory through her lashes.

"Would you care to sit and rest for awhile before we rejoin the others?"

She straightened. "I do think that would be best." She took the arm he offered and remembered to walk with a slight limp, since she was supposed to be temporarily lame.

Gregory led her back inside the room. For a moment,

Cassie remembered what had happened the last time they had been in this room. Just the recollection had her leg throbbing in truth.

Gregory led her to a chair and she sat down. "Would you care for something to drink?" he asked, referring to the sherry on the sideboard.

She barely withheld a shudder. "No, thank you. To be honest, I don't care to ever touch another drop of that poison ever again."

He offered a smile as the room fell silent. The tension that usually surrounded them when they were alone started to course through the room. Cassie's nerves began humming with anticipation, but Gregory's face was still a mask of calm indifference.

"You don't mind if I find something to read while I wait for you to recover, do you?" he asked.

"I..." That certainly hadn't been the reaction she'd been hoping for, but she schooled her features into a polite smile. "Of course."

He offered a brief nod, and then walked along the rows of novels. After a few minutes, he appeared to look closely at a particular title. "Hmm. This is interesting..." He started to remove the leather-bound volume from the shelf, only to have it stop halfway. A defined *click!* echoed throughout the room, followed by a slight whirring sound.

To Cassie's surprise, one half of the bookcase slid forward about two inches. Her mouth fell open, and she rushed over to the opening and peered into the inky black darkness beyond, the pretense of her pained appendage completely forgotten. "A secret passage! Rion told me that he'd never found any, that scoundrel!" She turned to Gregory. "Did you know about this?"

He didn't answer her query, but posed one of his own instead. "Do you want to see where it leads?"

"Yes!" *Is the man so dull-witted he can't see me practically jumping up and down in my excitement?*

Gregory walked over and pulled on the heavy oak shelving until the opening was large enough for them to walk through. A blast of cold air instantly overwhelmed her, along with the musty scent of disuse. She coughed and waved a hand in front of her face to clear the wave of dust. "It seems rather bleak, doesn't it?"

Gregory reached over her and grabbed an iron and glass lantern that was hanging on a nail on the passage wall. She held her breath as he turned back to her, his warm body only inches from her own. "This should help illuminate things," he said softly.

Cassie only nodded. She didn't trust herself to speak.

Gregory walked over to the desk and lit the half-melted tallow candle inside. He returned to her and held up the single, flickering light. He lifted a brow, his green eyes glittering. "Shall we?"

She clutched his jacket sleeve as they began to walk forward, but she was forced to keep her arms at her sides as they went deeper into the passageway. Cassie heard the slight drip of water echoing somewhere in the distance, and she didn't even want to know what sort of vermin might inhabit the cracks along those ancient walls.

She glanced back at the bookcase, now just a sliver of light behind them. As they turned a bend in the tunnel, they were plunged into darkness so deep that she wouldn't have been able to see her hand in front of her face if it wasn't for the flickering light that Gregory held. She prayed it held out.

"You have been here before, right?" she asked somewhat hesitantly.

"I'm not sure if it was this *particular* passage…"

Gregory's face was in shadow, but she swore she heard the grin in his voice. "That isn't funny," she warned. "I don't need to spend the rest of my life down here."

"Don't you trust me to find a way out if we got trapped?"

Cassie swallowed. Not only did she trust him with that, but with her very life as well. But since she couldn't very well tell him *that* without risking a broken heart in the bargain if he didn't return her sentiments, so she only warned him. "Just make sure you do."

The rumble of his deep chuckle surrounded them as it bounced off the cold stone. But instead of being ominous, the sound was comforting to Cassie.

It wasn't until they came to a fork in the passage that Gregory paused. "What is it?" Cassie whispered. "Don't tell me you don't know which way to *go*?"

"It's been a few years," was his reply.

"That isn't very comforting," she returned dryly.

He simply shrugged and turned left.

After what felt like an eternity trudging in the dark, during which time Cassie wondered if she had, indeed, underestimated Gregory's skill, they came to the end of the tunnel and faced a single wooden door. It was curved at the top and had iron bolts and hinges, and looked like something she imagined a medieval king might have in his castle.

She watched in fascination as Gregory felt around the edges of a stone next to the metal handle, and then he slowly pulled it free. From behind it he withdrew a single key and held it up to her. "Rion always keeps it locked."

She crossed her arms. "You knew where you were going all along, didn't you?"

He bent down and turned the key in the lock, and it freed the mechanism inside with a slight click. "I might have." He pushed open the door as he turned to her with a decidedly sheepish grin. He waved a hand. "After you."

Cassie glared at him as she passed, but once she entered the antechamber beyond, any scathing remarks that she might have hurled at Gregory's head promptly failed her. "It's...beautiful," she breathed.

Several silver candelabra were scattered about the

room, dozens of lit candles bathing the modest area in a warm glow. The area boasted a combination three red brick and gray stone archways, two of which were opposite one another, with worn tapestries hanging on the walls beyond. On the right side, she saw a small shelf of books and various odds and ends, while the left boasted a single table and two chairs.

But it was what lay beyond the archway in front of her, in the largest cavern, which held her fascination. A massive stone fireplace, with pillars framing it either side, took up the entire wall, the heat from the crackling fire making her sigh in appreciation, while a white fur rug lay before it.

It was obvious that Gregory had planned this little seduction scene. Which was rather ironic, since she'd been trying to think of a way to get *him* alone. She felt her lips twitch as she twirled to face him. She put her hands on her hips and asked coyly, "Are you trying to have your wicked way with me, Lord Gregory?"

"That depends." His voice was husky. "Is it working?" He cleared his throat and brought up arm up between them, revealing a sprig of mistletoe grasped in his fingers. "Then again," he added, "I did face the wrath of a fox to gain this little gem, after all."

She cocked her head to the side. "Ah, so I'm meant to kiss you out of obligation and gratitude, is that it?"

He winced. "I'd prefer it if I was granted a boon for another reason, like your hopeless attraction to me," he murmured. "But I'll take what I can get," he added with a decided twinkle in his eye.

Cassie wound her arms around his neck, plucking the mistletoe from his grasp and tossing it to the floor. "All you had to do was ask."

With that, she stood on her tiptoes and boldly placed her lips against his.

***

Gregory barely withheld a satisfied grin as he put his arms around Cassie's waist and drew her forward to deepen the kiss. He had laid his trap perfectly, having slipped away just before midnight to set up this entire seduction scene. But it was the trust Cassie had placed in him ever since he'd *found* the secret latch in the library that had been his undoing. He'd known without a doubt, in that moment, that he was going to marry her. There was no question in his mind on that score. In truth, there never really had been. Even though she might have frustrated him at every turn from the very first moment he'd met her, he knew their life together would never be boring.

He was confident that she felt the same, but tonight he would know for certain. Tonight, she would be his.

"Gregory..." She said his name on a pleading sigh, and any other thoughts promptly left his mind. The future could wait.

For now, nothing else mattered—but being with the woman he loved.

Chapter Nine

“I want you, Gregory.” Cassie could hardly believe that such demanding words had come out of her mouth. She hadn't meant to speak aloud; the words just came tumbling out. But already, the flames that Gregory had lit that day in her art studio now flared back to life, the fire threatening to consume her from the inside out.

“Are you sure?” he asked softly, his hand coming up to cup her cheek. “If we do this, there's no turning back. Do you understand that?”

“Yes, and I don't care.” She dared herself to meet his gaze, so that he could see the truth shining out of her eyes.

He smiled gently as he brushed a stray strand of hair out of her face. “My darling, Cassie,” he murmured.

He lightly kissed her lips, and then urged her to turn her back to him with a gentle pressure on her shoulder. Cassie's breathing turned shallow as Gregory slowly began to unbutton her gown. It was only after the green silk had fallen away and she stepped out of the pool of material at her feet did he start on her underclothes. She closed her eyes as he slowly unlaced her stays. Anticipation, mixed with maidenly apprehension, meshed together until she couldn't discern one from the other. The only thing she could focus on was Gregory's hands, as they traveled down the sides of her waist where only a thin cotton chemise covered her bare body.

He reached down and lifted the hem and slowly let his fingers trail back up her exposed skin, until he finally pulled the garment over her head and tossed it aside. Heart pounding, Cassied waited for him to turn her back to face him, but instead, he prolonged the torture by gently removing the pins from her hair. As the heavy mass of golden curls fell over her shoulders, she thought she heard him suck in a breath. In that moment, she realized that he was just as affected by her as she was by him.

When he brushed her hair aside and kissed the nape of her neck, a shiver traveled all the way down her spine. She closed her eyes and leaned her head back to give him better access. She moaned as his hands moved down her sides and around her ribcage. As his thumbs brushed her naked breasts, her heart nearly stopped. When he captured her nipples between his thumb and forefinger, rolling the hard pebbles between them, Cassie wavered on her feet, lightheaded with delirium.

His left hand remained on her breast, kneading and molding the soft flesh, while his right hand made a gentle path down her stomach and over her hip, until daring to brush the curls at the center of her core. When he rubbed a finger down her wet center, she jerked in surprise, the sensation both intimate and...*wanting.* When he started a steady rhythm, a strong sensation began to build within her. She pushed against his hand, her body acting on carnal instinct, but whatever it was she was searching for *needing*—it was just out of reach.

"You're so sweet, Cassie." Gregory's breath was hot

and harsh, but while his erotic murmurings went far to tease her, it wasn't until he thrust a finger inside of her did she finally come apart at the seams.

Her body shook as pleasure like nothing she'd ever felt before engulfed her in an erotic caress. Afterward, Gregory swept her up in his arms and carried her over to the fur rug where he gently laid her down.

He quickly divested himself of his clothes, his chest expanding with each breath he took. Cassie noticed the bulge in his trousers, gasping when his manhood to sprang free from its confines. Her eyes widened at the length and girth of him, but as he covered her body with his own, any virginal alarm she might have felt dissipated. He took his time loving her, his hands roaming, touching, teasing, and making her yearn for more.

She had never felt so comforted and safe—or *loved*— as she did right there.

With him.

"You're mine, Cassie. Forever."

He captured her mouth with his own, at the same time he thrust into her, breaking the final barrier that stood between them. She gasped at the initial intrusion, but as he slowly began to move, she began to relax. It was a strange feeling, yet she knew it was right. Being together, with Gregory, caused *so* many wonderful sensations to collide at once. But nothing was more satisfying than the feeling of being...complete. Whole.

With Gregory by her side, she knew that she wouldn't ever be lonely again.

As he increased his pace, she watched in fascination as he found his fulfillment, the sight of rapture on his face so overwhelming that she felt the happy sting of tears in her eyes.

***

Gregory pulled on his trousers and wrapped Cassie in his jacket, not because he didn't wish to continue to look his fill of her lovely form, but because he knew she might feel a little modest after what they'd shared. Above all else, he wanted her to be comfortable.

With him.

He pulled her into the crook of one arm. She rested her head on his chest while he ran his other hand gently down her hair. He had never felt more relaxed or sated in his entire life. If he hadn't already known that he loved Cassie and wanted to spend the rest of his life with her, he would have admitted it now, for anywhere she was, he knew it would feel like home.

"I wish we could stay here forever," she whispered. "Our own personal haven."

He had to smile, for she had mirrored his exact sentiment. But since he didn't want to get overly emotional, he said, "Actually, it was my secret hideout with Rion when I came to visit. He knew that you wouldn't be able to find us here."

"Cretin," she grumbled, and his grin widened. "I intend to give him a piece of my mind."

"But if you do that," he pointed out, "then we might not be able to sneak in here again."

"Now *that* is a terrible thought." Cassie sighed and snuggled closer.

Gregory closed his eyes. He would enjoy this moment just a bit longer. After that, they would return to the reality that awaited them beyond the door. But he had to admit that it didn't look too bleak after tonight.

***

A firm pounding jerked Gregory wide-awake. It took him a moment to figure out what was happening, but when memory slammed back into him and he started to sit up, he remembered why his left arm was heavy and numb. A beautiful woman curled up next to him. If it was possible, Cassie was even lovelier in repose. Unfortunately, he had to rouse her. Rather quickly, if Rion's irritated shout meant anything on the other side of that door.

"Gregory! Dammit, answer me if you're in there!"

He winced. *This isn't good.* He was about to be found in what might as well be *in flagrante delicto* with Cassie, which didn't bother Gregory in the slightest, since he intended to make an honest woman out of her. He just didn't want her reputation to be pelted with unnecessary slurs, or his face pummeled with unnecessary fists from her brother.

"Just a minute!" he called out, finally causing Cassie to stir. He couldn't resist giving her a light kiss as her eyes fluttered open. "Wake up, my love. We have company."

"What's going on?" Rion demanded. "Why haven't you opened this door?"

Cassie instantly bolted upright. "It's Rion!" she hissed in alarm. She scrambled to her feet and began to gather her clothes. "God, what time is it? Oh, I can't find my other stocking!" She glanced at Gregory with wide, fearful blue eyes. "He sounds terribly angry. What are we going to do?"

Gregory wanted nothing more than to reassure her, to say that everything was going to be fine, but he knew that Rion was impatient enough not to wait for a romantic proposal. Instead, he was just going to have to deal with the brunt of his friend's anger until he was given a chance to explain, and find the right time to ask permission for Cassie's hand.

He stood up. "I'm going to open the door," he said calmly. He heard Cassie's horrified gasp as he went over and unlatched the lock. He was glad he'd had the foresight to lock it earlier, or else Rion would have gained an eyesight more than he'd bargained for should he have barged right in—rather like he did the moment.

"What the hell are you doing in here?" Rion paced the room. He looked frazzled. "I've been looking all over for you! A messenger arrived not twenty minutes past—" He abruptly broke off as he happened to look beyond Gregory's shoulder.

Gregory didn't have to follow Rion's gaze. He had a good idea how Cassie might appear—blond hair in disarray, clothes a complete dishabille, cheeks pink with embarrassment and perhaps a touch of guilt.

He was so content with the image of her in his mind that it didn't hurt nearly as bad as he thought it might when Rion smashed his fist into his jaw. But since he'd been waiting for the blow, expecting it really, he only stumbled backward.

"Rion, *stop!*"

Gregory heard Cassie rush over to intercede, but he held out a hand to her without taking his eyes off her incensed brother. "Stay out of it, Cassie," he said quietly.

"I thought you were my friend," Rion spat. "I didn't believe that you would actually go behind my back and take advantage of my sister like this."

Gregory absorbed all the barbs Rion shot at him. After all, it wouldn't be the first time he'd stood by and allowed Rion to expend his anger. And this time, he knew it was deserved.

***

Cassie didn't care if Gregory had ordered her to stay out of their argument, especially since it concerned *her.* She refused to stay silent any longer.

"That's enough!" she shouted at Rion, stepping between him and Gregory. While she hadn't been able to tighten the laces of her stays or her gown, at least she was decent, and with Gregory's discarded jacket on, one might not even tell she wasn't fully clothed. "I forgave you for one idiotic fight already, but I won't do it again."

Rion's furious blue eyes shifted to her. She had never seen such rage emanating from him. "He *violated* you, Cassie." He enunciated each word carefully, as if she might have a hard time understanding the severity of the situation otherwise. "You know what this could do to your reputation should anyone find out. It will be your ruin."

She set her hands on her hips. "First of all, he did not *violate* me. This may be difficult for you to comprehend, but I gave myself to Gregory *willingly*." Her brother's head jerked back as if she'd struck him. "Secondly, no one will find out unless *you* tell them. But either way, if the truth does come out, I'm prepared to accept the consequences of my actions, because I love him. Do you hear me, Rion Ashcroft?" She poked her finger in the middle of his chest. "I *love* him, and if you dare to strike him again I will never forgive you."

Once Cassie was finished with her tirade, Rion blinked, as if coming out of a haze. His shoulders slumped. "I'm sorry, Cass. I didn't think—" He swallowed.

"Then perhaps you need to learn to *start*," she snapped.

Rion gave a brief bob of his head, and then turned to offer a hand to Gregory. He hesitated briefly, but then accepted the olive branch, the only thing that stood for an apology from Rion.

After a moment, Rion shook his head, as if something had jarred loose. "I nearly forgot." He took a missive out of his pocket and handed it to Gregory. "A messenger arrived from Bath a short time ago. Your father has taken ill and has requested your immediate presence."

Chapter Ten

Eleven days passed without a single word from Gregory.

Cassie did her best to smile and participate in the activities that her cousins had planned for the duration of their stay, but her heart just wasn't in anything. In spite of her melancholy, when she had a moment to slip away to her art room, she took it.

She tried to tell herself that Gregory was honorable, but considering he hadn't even bothered to send a note letting them know how things were faring with the baron, her hope that he might return to offer for her was starting to fade.

"I don't see how you can stand it in here. It's so... quiet," Agnes drawled as she walked into the room where Cassie was busy working on her latest landscape project.

Cassie shrugged. "I like it." She let Agnes ramble on as she continued to paint a cheery blue sky.

"In case you've been too busy to notice, today is Twelfth Night, and the last day we shall all be together, likely for some time." Agnes paused, as if waiting for Cassie to add to the conversation. When she received more silence, she continued, "We are planning to go wassailing in the village this evening, and we've decided that you are going to be the honorary queen."

"Indeed?" Cassie murmured, knowing she was expected to respond.

"And do you want to know who the king is?" Agnes added.

Cassie sighed. "Who?" She honestly couldn't have cared less. She just wanted to stay there and wallow in her self-pity. She definitely didn't want to attend some ridiculous celebration to the trees, but it appeared as though she might not have a choice.

"Why, your favorite person in the whole world, of course."

Cassie finally set aside her brush and turned to face Rion. Her first genuine smile of the day touched her lips. "Are you sure about that?"

Agnes had the good sense to know that they needed some privacy, but even so, she blew Rion a frustrating kiss on her way out.

He merely rolled his eyes, and then turned his attention back to Cassie.

They hadn't spoke more than a handful of words to each other since he'd discovered her and Gregory in the secret room. Whether it was an unspoken agreement to not discuss it after Gregory's departure, or Rion was just giving her some space until she was ready to talk about it, Cassie wasn't sure. But considering the contemplative expression on her brother's face now, she knew her time had finally run out.

"I hope we're still friends, Cass," he said, uncertainly.

Her heart thawed a bit. "Rion—"

"Wait." He held up a hand. "Just…let me say what I came here to say."

Cassie clasped her hands in her lap. And waited patiently.

He blew out a breath as he shoved his hands in his pockets. "This is harder than I thought it would be," he muttered, although he pushed on. "I'm not really...good at the mushy stuff, Cass. I don't really even know what to say, except that I hope you'll join us tonight. I feel like you're trying to become some princess in her tower, just waiting for the moment when her true love comes to her rescue." He clenched his jaw, his annoyance toward Gregory portrayed in that single action. "I know you think I'm too young to understand a bruised heart, but I'm not. Not really."

He swallowed hard, his voice turning husky. "When our parents died, I was devastated. I still have a...difficult time with it. I know someday I'll be able to face the fact they're gone. But not yet. I'm sorry, Cass. I just can't...see them yet."

Cassie felt her eyes well with tears. The fact that he was opening up to her like this was all she'd ever wanted.

He ran a hand through his dark hair. "The point is, I feel I'm always doing more harm than good when it comes to the people I care about most. I know you're my sister, but I don't want to lose you as a friend." He looked away, and in that moment, he appeared so young and lost that the rest of the icy shell that had closed around Cassie's heart cracked completely. "If you don't want to play the part of the queen, I understand, but I'd really appreciate it if you would at least...join the rest of us. Don't let the idiotic prince, who was supposed to save the day, ruin it instead."

Tears were streaming down Cassie's face by that point. She stood on unsteady legs and walked over to him. She pressed a hand to her chest. "You're my brother, Rion, and I'll love you until the day I die. I would be honored to stand by your side as your queen. You should know, by now, that I would stand by your side through anything."

She reached out and hugged him. As she sobbed, she could have sworn that she heard a rather suspicious sniff of his own.

***

That evening, Cassie was surprised to see not only the cousins, but every single guest at Ashcroft Hall—young and old—was dressed in his or her best and warmest attire. They were milling about in the foyer, ready to head out, but when someone spied her descending the stairs, there was a loud whistle followed by a near deafening round of applause. It wasn't until Phoebe came over with a crown made of laurel and holly, and the crowd instantly hushed, that Cassie felt a blush steal across her cheeks as she realized the reason for her sudden popularity.

She was the Queen of Twelfth Night.

Phoebe offered her a wink, and then she cleared her throat and said in all seriousness, "It has been decided, by these assembled, that you are the chosen queen to bring forth health and prosperity to the dormant apple trees in the village, so that they may thrive and ensure a good harvest this autumn." She held up the crown of evergreen. "We present this token of our appreciation during your reign, Your Majesty."

Phoebe gently laid the crown atop Cassie's bare head. After that, she was presented with a green velvet cloak, which Cousin Nicholas wrapped around her shoulders. Jeffrey was the next to approach, carrying a cup in both hands like a sacrificial offering. With a roll of his eyes, he handed it over to Phoebe, who must have been the designated "mistress of ceremonies."

Cassie had to struggle to hold back a smile. She knew they had done all this in an effort to cheer her spirits.

Phoebe gestured for one of the younger cousins, who was about five years of age, to come forward. "Jacob will be our 'Tom Tit,' who has the honor of placing a slice of cider-soaked toast on a single branch in each tree in the village orchard in order to deter any bad spirits that might be lurking after the Christmas season. But first, we ask that our queen bless this cup of wassail, so that our celebrations may commence."

Cassie obediently took a drink of the spiced cider, the warm liquid creating a path to her stomach. "Where is the 'king'?" she asked, for she had yet to see Rion. She wondered how he'd managed to get out of partaking in these rituals.

"He's waiting for you outside." Phoebe grinned, with a dramatic wave of her hand toward the front door.

Cassie walked forward, the assemblage around her parting like Moses dividing the Red Sea. She held back a giggle and though they were exaggerating the importance of these old folklore rites—until she walked outside.

And saw who was dressed as the king.

She couldn't move. She couldn't *breathe*.

All she could do was stare at Gregory, who stood at the base of the stone steps and looked up at her. The darkness around them was silent and still, the only light flickering from the house and the twinkling stars in the heavens, but still, she only had eyes for him.

He looked absolutely resplendent in a snowy white cravat and bottle green jacket that she knew would match his eyes to perfection. Impeccably polished Hessians covered the lower half of his legs, complimenting the black trousers he wore, hugging thighs that she knew were just as muscular as they appeared. His light brown hair was slightly tousled, and the crown of laurel and holly on his head matched hers exactly.

"Hello, Cassie."

She closed her eyes against the pull of that hypnotic voice. Had it really only been a fortnight ago that she had been dreading the thought of him coming to Ashcroft Hall?

Now, he was here, yet again, and her heart felt as though it was slowly shattering in her chest.

"I haven't heard from you in almost two weeks." She hoped that he could hear how broken she had been.

"I'm sorry, Cassie. I should have sent word long before now—" He sighed heavily. "My father died the day I arrived in Bath. I had to escort my mother home and take care of a few estate matters…" His voice trailed off and a tight expression crept over his face. "I know that doesn't excuse my actions, only that you might understand the circumstances a bit better and why it has taken me so long to return."

"I would have been there for you if I had only known," she whispered, her heart breaking for his loss.

"I know," he replied softly. "But what you don't understand is that you *were* with me." He took a step upward toward her, and another, and another, until he stood directly in front of her. "While I've been in hell these past few days, there was one bright moment, and that was the thought of seeing you again. And going home so I could get this."

He bent down on one knee and pulled a red velvet box from his pocket. He lifted the lid.

Cassie couldn't seem to tear her eyes away from the sparkling ring revealed in his grasp. It was a perfect emerald, surrounded by diamonds.

"This was my grandmother's wedding ring. I hope that it will now grace the hand of my bride-to-be. That is—" His mouth kicked up at the corner. "—if she will have me after all my blunders and mistakes."

Her eyes shifted to his, where they were glowing with hope, but more importantly, with love. "Lady Cassiopeia Brumhilda Agnes Mildred Ashcroft, I love you with every beat of my heart. Will you do me the honor of accepting my hand and becoming my wife, and the next Baroness Ambrel?"

A sob escaped Cassie, and she covered her mouth with her hand. She tried to speak, but her throat had closed up from an emotion so deep that it spilled out of her eyes and began to course down her cheeks. She finally managed to nod.

The grin that appeared on his face lit up the night sky as he removed the emerald ring and slid it onto the third finger of her left hand. It glittered with a brilliant light, but she didn't think it could rival the love shining out of Gregory's eyes. "I love you, too."

With that, he pulled her into his arms where they shared a kiss to seal their bargain.

***

"Well, I daresay that took long enough, did it not?" Isabel held Mr. Pugglesworth in her arms. She stood at the window of the front parlor, her grandson at her side. "But then young Gregory can be just as stubborn as you at times, Rion, dear."

Rion crossed his arms and turned to regard his grandmother with a dry smile. "I doubt that."

She couldn't help but chuckle as she turned away from the happy couple on her front steps. She sat down on the settee and stroked her pug's back, eliciting a happy whine from the animal. Unfortunately, he still wouldn't go near that wool scarf, even after her best efforts to persuade him that it was harmless.

"You better go join the others," she said to Rion. "I doubt they will be content to wait for long before they set out to join the villagers in their excursions, especially now that Gregory's plan was executed so perfectly."

"I suppose I should." He gave a long-suffering sigh. "Even if I have to deal with Agnes' constant chattering, and Gregory and Cassie mooning over each other."

"I wouldn't scoff too much if I were you," Isabel

warned. "For someday you may find yourself in a very similar situation."

Rion rolled his eyes. "The day I let a female turn me into some sappy-eyed idiot is the day I pawn the Couleur Magnifique. Which will be *never*." He emphasized the last.

As he strode out of the room, Isabel glanced after him with a secret smile, a sure sign that an idea was beginning to take root in her mind…

Epilogue

London, England
Fourteen years later

"It's the perfect plan, Cass. Surely you can see that."

Rion paced the length of the Ambrel House parlor, his focus intent and so determined that his sister knew there was no hope of dissuading him. Not even her dear husband, Gregory, had managed to talk any sense into his former school comrade.

Unfortunately, what Rion proposed *would* help her. With a pair of toddler twins and a babe on the way at any time, she was feeling the draining effects of pregnancy since her governess had departed her post on a family emergency. Family came first though, so Cassie had reluctantly bid her former employee farewell with her best wishes and a promise to give her a recommendation should she choose to seek another post in the future. But now, of course, that left her in something of a desperate situation—

one that her brother fully intended to exploit in order to retrieve a missing family heirloom.

Cassie sighed. These were the times when she missed her grandmother's counsel. She would know what to say to make it all better. Sadly, the dowager countess had quietly passed away in her sleep some months ago. After the death of her beloved pug shortly before that, it had seemed as though that had been the last loss Isabel had been willing to endure on this earth.

Cassie could only hope that wherever her grandmother was now, she was looking down and watching over them, because she wasn't sure that she could deal with Rion on her own anymore. She loved her brother now as much as she ever had, but only a miracle would turn that brittle shell of a heart into something solid and unbreakable.

Only true love could make the difference.

Until that special lady came along and freed Rion from his personal chains, all Cassie could do was wait.

And pray.

About the Author

Tabetha Waite is the multi-award winning author of the historical romance Ways of Love Series. Her debut novel, "Why the Earl is After the Girl," was published in July of 2016 and won the 2017 Best Indie Book Award in Romance and the 2018 Second Place Feathered Quill Book Award in Romance. She is a certified PAN member of the RWA. When she's not writing, Tabetha is reading as true bookworms do, or checking out any antique mall she comes across. During the school year she works as a lunch attendant at the local community college. She is a small town, Missouri girl and continues to make her home in the Midwest with her husband and two wonderful daughters.

You can find her on most any social media site, and she encourages fans of her work to join her mailing list for updates.

www.authortabethawaite.wix.com/romance

Made in the USA
Las Vegas, NV
30 December 2021

39843179R00059